# The Arcane Heart

**Thrall Prince Romance, Volume 3**

Caroline Gibson

Published by Caroline Gibson, 2020.

This is a work of fiction. Similarities to real people, places, or events are entirely coincidental.

THE ARCANE HEART

**First edition. May 15, 2020.**



Written by Caroline Gibson.

# Pull

Prince Lonn strode through the Varhin market, the thud of his boots and his dark glare scattering people from his path.

He hated this place; it was filled with nothing but filth, misery and thieves. Today, though, he had been drawn to it. Something that had pulled him to this place, something underneath the stench and noise that impelled him to search through the stalls and booths. He did not understand the compulsion, but he trusted his instincts, and he could not ignore it.

He let his feet take him to the back of the Varhin, where less legal and less savory goods were traded. It was no secret on Tornatt that the Varhin market allowed dealing in low magics, stolen artifacts, and slaves. Otharn tolerated it, as it was not done too openly, the traders did not cross anyone of note, and most importantly, they paid their regular tributes on time and without complaint. Lonn was a prince of Otharn; he knew how the worlds worked.

At the very back of the market, Lonn's steps slowed. Here, rough curtains enclosed most of the stalls. Few showed their wares openly. The pull on Lonn's awareness increased, a sensation unlike any he had ever felt before. His every nerve dragged him in one direction, bending his path towards the source. He was drawn forward as if by a magnet, by a gravitational field, by a deep, dizzying well that he could not help but peer into. His armed escort drew closer around him, but his captain, Hilde, did not speak or question her prince.

Lonn turned slowly on his heel, as though scenting the air. He paused, then walked toward a dim doorway, one among many. He knew it was the right one. Silently, Hilde darted before him and entered first, taking up a position by the door. Her keen eyes flicked to all corners of the space to check for threats in the scant moments before her prince entered.

It was a miserable place. The crystals that should have lit the cramped space were dim, some even completely dark. Only a low place indeed could not afford charged crystal lamps to provide light and warmth. This very market sold them for pennies apiece. The floor was unswept, the air stale and chill, and tattered cloth concealed half of the space.

Lonn tapped his foot and looked around. The pull was stronger than ever here, like a thread wound through his heart, but he could see nothing that might have spun such a thread. For the first time, unease crossed his mind. Was some unfriendly force at play, compelling him to this place? Was this an ambush, a trap? Hilde obviously shared his concern, and her hand lingered by the hilt of her weapon. Her second-in-command, Lieutenant Ake, stepped into the booth and took up a position on Lonn's left, his face tense under his thick beard.

Moments passed, one thudding heartbeat after another. Lonn held up a hand for everyone to wait. Something was coming, bubbling up beneath the surface, about to break through. They stood in bated silence until shuffling footsteps preceded a hooded figure from behind the curtain. The light from the sputtering lamps did not illuminate the figure's face. The hood was pulled down low, and a voluminous robe fell to the floor, concealing any hint of an identity. The figure looked at the three of them in turn, Lonn last, seemingly unimpressed by the tall prince standing in the pitiful emporium.

"I know what you are here to buy," the figure said, the gravelly voice scratchy but unmistakably female. "You are almost too late."

Lonn tasted copper in the air; the woman's natural magic, uncontrolled, was touching him, looking for a foothold, searching for a way in. This was the height of ill-manners, and Lonn did not hesitate to shove it back. He was no trained sorcerer like his brother Vell, but he had natural strength and the ability to channel magic from the crystal realm. He would not tolerate such blatant disrespect from this strange woman. Her magic was weak, and he felt no resistance when he pushed it away.

"If you know why I am here, do not waste any more of my time," Lonn said, impatient. He was eager to be gone from this place. It made his skin crawl, but he could not leave until he had found the force that had summoned him here. The woman laughed, twisted and mocking, and pulled back the curtain to reveal what was in the cramped space behind.

Lonn's lip turned up in disgust. Behind the curtain, inside a filthy, confined cage was a man. The light blue of his skin told Lonn that he was from Fryst, a semi-rebellious world within Otharn's protectorate. The man looked starved, his cheeks hollow, his skin blotchy. He huddled in the corner of his cage with knees drawn up, arms wrapped around himself, but he stared up at Lonn as the prince approached, his eyes a deep, dark blue. Lonn knew at once that the man was the source of the strange pull. It was even stronger now, drawing him closer to the cage. He crouched, and the Fryst man did not look away, meeting Lonn's gaze despite his obvious exhaustion.

"Help me," the man said. His voice was a rough whisper, but his gaze did not waver. "I was kidnapped from my world and brought here against my will. Help me, please."

Lonn didn't answer, although he was sure the man spoke the truth. Less than a quarter of the joined worlds allowed the trading of slaves, and Fryst was not among them. Whoever this man was, he was no lawful slave. Lonn touched the bars of the cage, unsurprised to feel wards thrumming through the metal. He could break them, given enough time and freedom from interference, but Lonn had a tickling suspicion that this woman was more than she seemed. He would proceed with caution.

"I have no use for a half-dead slave," he declared, forcing himself to stand and step back, his teeth clenched with the effort of it.

"Indeed," the cloaked woman replied, "surely you do not. Why then, did you come here?"

The presence of the man in the cage was burning into Lonn's senses. His natural magic pulled at him like a dog on a leash, stronger than he had ever felt it, desperate to be close, to twist around the man and soothe and protect him. Lonn controlled it. He would swear it did not show on his face, but the woman cocked her cloaked head at him, knowing.

Lonn ground his teeth. This woman knew she had something special in her trap, something that would summon a magic user such as himself to bargain with her. He would not get the man out of her clutches cheaply, but he was not unfamiliar with negotiation, having sat with his father at many a treaty table. He would not name a price before she did.

"It has been three days," the woman said, her harsh voice low. "I would suggest you do not delay. How much longer do you think he can survive without food or water?"

Lonn's temper flared at her words, her ruthlessness. He had little idea how long Fryst people could last without eating or drinking, but judging by the man's appearance it would not be much longer. Lonn glanced back to the cage. The man's desperate blue eyes were still on him, but half-lidded now, as though the effort of maintaining his gaze was too much. He did not speak again. Perhaps he judged that getting out of the cage was more important than protesting the fact that he was in it. Lonn could sense the man's heartbeat, his natural magic pulsing in time with it, dangerously labored.

"Release him, woman," he growled, his anger rising as the heartbeat slowed. He stepped towards her, grabbing a handful of her robes in his clenched fist. The woman gasped and a poorly cast repulsion spell sputtered and failed under Lonn's fingers where they twisted in her robe. Lonn was no mage, but he was protected from such feeble tricks by the strength of his connection to the crystal realm. Arcane energy filled him, soaked into his very bones. It defended itself, and him.

"Release him, or I will strike you down!" Lonn shoved the witch away, and she flew back, hitting the wall with a bitten-back moan of pain, her body lighter than Lonn had expected. Despite her fall, her hood was not dislodged. Even her hands were covered by black gloves. Not an inch of flesh showed.

"I will sell him to you," she offered hastily, scrambling back to her feet.

Lonn nodded, his face like thunder. Perhaps the witch finally understood the seriousness of her situation. She might have somehow acquired a cage with powerful wards, but her weak castings had little use here. She was overpowered, and she should take her chance to escape with a few coins and her head still on her shoulders. Lonn would claim his prize from her, he had no doubt about that.

She named a price, and Lonn laughed out loud. Perhaps his father could empty his vaults and pay such a price, but for a random magic-user, even a wealthy one such as she took him to be, it was ridiculous. He folded his arms and waited. He would not counter such an offer. Let her argue herself to a reasonable price. It was a strategy his ever-patient brother had shared with him. People hate silence and will scramble to fill it. If you can remain silent long enough, the person across the table will start to negotiate on your behalf.

Sure enough, she relented after less than half a minute.

"Very well," she said, and named a far more reasonable rate, adding, "And you will owe me one favor."

Lonn pushed on her price. He offered different quantities of gems, precious metals, artifacts, until both were satisfied with the deal. He had enough funds to cover the purchase without needing to sell anything that would cause his mother, Queen Anlira, to question him. He cared little about the favor. He would pay her child's dowry or find an apprenticeship for them or get the witch out of whatever jail she inevitably ended up in. Whatever she decided to ask for. It was no matter to him.

The witch glided forward, her haughty demeanor restored at their successful negotiation. She turned back the sleeve of her robe and tugged off her glove to reveal a hand already glittering with oath-magic.

"Swear to it, then," the witch said.

Lonn clasped her hand without hesitation, biting back a hiss as the magic burrowed into his arm, binding them both to the oath. One Fryst slave, in exchange for a good amount of coin and one favor. The oath magic was strong, and Lonn was unsettled the power of the bond compared to the witch's feeble attempt at repulsion. The witch's skin felt rough under Lonn's hand and he looked down, surprised. Her hand and arm were livid with burns, some scarred over but most still red and raw. *No wonder she covered herself,* Lonn thought, *if the rest of her looks like that.*

As soon as the bond <u>completed</u>, the cage door clicked and swung open. Lonn's magical energy rushed inside, toward the Fryst man, eager to be close to him, to connect with him and envelop him. Lonn reeled as the tendrils of his magic found their target. He kept his feet by force of will, refusing to let the slaver-woman see him in a weakened state. He crouched again by the cage, his head spinning with the force of his magic as it swirled around the man. The man was still conscious, but barely, and Lonn half-helped, half-dragged him out of the cage, steadying him as he stumbled, weak from days without sustenance. Lonn needed to take him to his garrison camp where he could rest and recover. Without a backward glance at the witch, Lonn and his new possession left the booth.

# Fate

The man was barely standing. His eyes fluttered closed every few seconds, his lips were cracked and dry. Lonn's escort closed in, all studiously avoiding staring at the bedraggled slave their prince had for some reason purchased.

"Water," the man said, his voice a bare whisper.

Lonn was angry at himself for not immediately taking care of the man's needs. Ake offered a bottle and Lonn snatched it, holding it steady for him to drink. That vile woman had said he had been three days in the cage without food or water. It was a miracle he was conscious, never mind standing and speaking. Lonn's magic tugged at him, wanting to get closer to the man, wanting to bury itself within him, but Lonn held it back as best he could. Now was not the time.

The man handed back the bottle, and in the same movement stepped to the side and put his back to the nearest wall. He reached over his shoulder, as though seeking a weapon, but nothing was there. His movement took him out of the circle of guards, a defensive strategy that Lonn approved of. Clearly, this man was no fool. Lonn waved his guards away and let the man have his space.

"Where are we?" the man asked, rubbing his face as though trying to force himself to stay awake.

"This is Tornatt," Lonn told him. "We are at the Varhin market, about half a day's ride from the capital city. You have no need to be afraid. I mean you no harm."

The man did not look convinced at that, and Lonn did not blame him one bit. If he had been kidnapped, starved, taken to another planet and sold, and was now weaponless and surrounded by armed guards, he would not feel safe either. He tried to set the man at ease. "Will you tell me your name?" he asked, moving closer to the Fryst man, worried that he would collapse at any moment.

"Llias," the man answered, staggering and leaning on the wall for support, "My name is Llias."

Lonn held out his hand to Ake and took the small package of food he knew the man would have ready. Ake was a healer as well as a warrior, and he was nothing if not reliable.

"Here," Lonn said, opening the bundle and showing Llias the nuts and dried fruit inside, "Eat something."

Llias looked longingly at the food, and Lonn could see the indecision on his face. To ease his mind, he grabbed a few of the nuts himself and crunched them between his teeth, then held out the food again. Llias took it.

"My thanks," he said, his mouth already full.

"We should leave," Hilde said, her eyes scanning the increasingly disreputable-looking market around them. "It is late, and this is no place to linger by night."

Lonn agreed. The Varhin by day was bad enough. He had no desire to be present for the night trade.

"Come," he said to Llias, holding out an arm to him, "We will go to my garrison, and you can rest."

Llias swallowed his mouthful of food and shook his head, his dark eyes never leaving Lonn's face, evaluating his reaction to his words. "Thank you," he said, "But I must return to Fryst at once. I have been gone from my responsibilities too long already."

Lonn's every instinct rebelled at the idea of Llias leaving. Under his skin, the prince's arcane power boiled and churned, seeking the warmth and comfort of Llias' touch. Lonn tried not to show it, but Llias gave him a quizzical look, as though he could sense something, and pressed himself further back against the wall. Lonn was staring, and it was unsettling the man, but he could not stop himself.

"The nearest portal site is beyond the garrison," Hilde interjected, breaking the tension between the two of them.

Hilde was clearly keen to be gone from this place, and unsure as to why her prince was acting so strangely. It was unlike Lonn to care about a prisoner, even one as unusual and exotic as this Fryst man.

"The weather is bad, and night is falling," she continued, an edge of impatience in her voice. "Come to the garrison with us and decide there what to do next."

It was a practical suggestion, and Llias could do little but agree. If he did not come with them, where else would he go? If he lingered in the Varhin in his present state, he would no doubt find himself in a worse situation than if he went with Lonn. At least Lonn was reasonably polite and had given him food and water.

Llias nodded and pushed off from the wall, his steps unsteady. He waved away the offer of Lonn's arm.

"I can walk," he said, leaning on the walls as he passed.

Lonn ground his teeth as he watched his unsteady progress. He longed to help, his magic pulling at him to support the man, to protect him and care for him, but he held back. It would be unwelcome, and he was not so uncouth as that. Instead, he followed as closely as he dared. He ignored the looks from his guards. There was something special about Llias, some connection that his magic sought out, and he did not know what it was. Until he discovered its cause, he would keep the man close. There was nothing wrong with that, and if his guards had any opinion about it, they would be wise not to express it.

Llias' steps grew more unsteady as they reached the entrance. He leaned on the walls and stumbled over his own feet — which, as Lonn saw with another lurch of rage, were bare. The witch had even taken his shoes! Lonn jumped every time Llias tripped, ready to catch him if he fell. Llias seemed grimly determined to make it without assistance, but Lonn was sure he would not. They were far underground, and the long, steep ramp back up to the surface would surely defeat him, even if the walk to the ramp did not.

"What is your name, Commander?" Llias asked, his blue skin pale, and his breath coming in shallow gasps.

Lonn had not introduced himself; he was used to being recognized wherever he went. But he had never been to Fryst, and the Fryst were not allowed to travel freely among the joined worlds, by order of the king. Lonn was wearing Otharnian armor and the gold sunburst insignia of a commander, not the crown insignia of a prince. He was not even wearing his signature sky-blue cape, opting for stealth instead of pomp. No wonder Llias did not know him, and Lonn was glad to think that the witch probably did not know him either. If she thought him some mid-ranking member of the Otharnian military, she would be less eager to claim her favor than if she knew he was a prince.

"I am Prince Lonn of Otharn," he told Llias, "Son of King Covl."

Llias' eyes widened, and despite himself he grabbed Lonn's arm to stay upright as he staggered. When he got his breath back and released Lonn's arm, he said, "You are the crown prince? What are you doing here? Why did you come to find me?"

Lonn shrugged, sure that the answer was more complicated than he knew. "Perhaps it was fate," he suggested, thinking of the mysterious summons he had felt, and the way his magic fought to connect with this man. Llias huffed out a pained laugh, white teeth flashing against blue lips.

"You Otharnians and your fate," he said, "On Fryst we would call it luck."

"Aye, maybe so," Lonn said with an answering laugh. Llias' weak smile was enough to lighten his spirits and ease his worry. "Perhaps it *was* luck that led me to find you."

Llias' good humor did not last. Before they reached the ramp, he was stumbling with every step, his eyes half closed, his head hanging low. He still stubbornly refused help, so Ake ghosted up beside him, ready to catch him when he fell.

It did not take long.

The ramp was within sight when Llias crumpled soundlessly. Ake and Lonn grabbed him before he hit the ground, and Ake called two guards forward to carry him the rest of the way.

"No," Lonn said, pulling Llias' limp form away from Ake and hoisting him in his own arms. "I will take him."

Ake pursed his lips under his thick beard and frowned. "Aye, my prince. As you wish."

Llias was a solid weight in Lonn's arms, but the prince hardly felt it. The joyous churn of his arcane energy was strong where Llias' skin touched his own; it powered his muscles and lightened his steps. Lonn carried Llias up the ramp without faltering, ignoring the looks he got from the passersby and from his own guards. The unconscious man's arms fell to his sides, his torn shirt falling open to reveal his pale blue skin. An angry slash curved down the center of his chest, and there was another deeper one on his side, slicing down over his hip. They looked recent, and painful. A remnant of his capture, most likely. Lonn pulled his eyes away from Llias' exposed skin. He was beyond intrigued by the man, but this was not the time or place to be following such thoughts.

It was raining and cold outside the Varhin, the stars hidden beneath thick clouds. As soon as they were under the open sky, Lonn summoned Skarpur to his hand.

"I will return to the garrison," he declared, hoisting Llias' limp form over his shoulder. "Join me there."

"Yes, my prince," Hilde said.

She clearly wanted to say more, but Lonn did not give her time. Llias needed to rest, to be safe and cared for, and that was not going to happen out on the cold, wet plain outside the Varhin market.

Lonn let everything fall away. Every worry and stress and unfinished task that preyed on his mind, whether regarding Llias, his family or his work here on Tornatt. He would deal with all that later, but for now he only had to do one thing: He held up his spear, kicked off from the ground, and flew.

In the darkness behind them, a hooded figure watched. The witch raised her hand in a mocking wave, the glimmer of oath magic still shining. "I will see you soon, Prince," she whispered as Lonn and his unconscious burden vanished into the driving rain.

# Care

The surge of energy through Skarpur took Lonn's breath away. The spear was an ancient artifact, linked to the power of the crystal realm by great mages of the past. It had been wielded by generations of the Otharnian royal family, its strength increasing with each one. Skarpur always answered Lonn's command, but now the power flowed without any resistance. The energy was not so much summoned as bursting through of its own accord. Lonn and Llias soared easily, wind and rain whipping around them. Even with Llias on his shoulder, Lonn was as steady as if standing on solid ground. His spirits rose, and even the rain soaking them both could not dampen his exhilaration.

The circle of lights of the sprawling garrison appeared under them within only a few minutes. Lonn touched down in his own camp, backed up against the mountains and set apart from the four companies of soldiers he commanded. The rain beat down, turning the bare earth to mud, and the surprised guards came running.

"Who goes there?" they demanded, weapons drawn, before recognizing their prince.

"Fetch hot water and dry clothes," Lonn ordered, tossing Skarpur in the air to dissolve into golden sparks.

He carried Llias inside his spacious tent and laid him on his bed, careful not to scrape any of the former prisoner's injuries. A few minutes of anxious pacing later, a guard appeared in the entrance with the supplies he had requested.

It was Nife, one of Lonn's younger guards. He was newly appointed and eager to prove himself; he must have run all the way to the cooks' tent on the far side of the garrison to get the jug of steaming water he carried.

Nife looked anxiously at the unconscious man on the prince's bed, taking in his ragged clothes, his open shirt, his injuries.

"May I assist you, my prince?" he asked, wisely swallowing whatever other questions he might have had. "Shall I fetch a healer?"

"No healer," Lonn said. The very idea of anyone but him touching Llias was unacceptable.

"Yes, my prince," Nife said. He shuffled his feet and looked back at Llias again before he cleared his throat and added, "Lieutenant Ake has a healing kit in his tent..."

"Fetch it," Lonn ordered, and Nife vanished.

In the dimly lit tent, Lonn pulled the blanket up to cover Llias, leaving his injured side uncovered. He set his hand to Llias' forehead, relieved to find he was not feverish. Letting the touch linger, he dwelled on the connection growing between them. Lonn's palm tingled, the arcane energy in his body surging to that point, trying to bridge the gap. The connection was weak, but warm. It drew Lonn in, promised something that Lonn didn't yet understand, but that he wanted.

Lonn was still standing there when Nife returned with the healing kit and a cup of warm broth. He blinked at Lonn, unsure as to what he was doing, unsure about the man the prince held in such regard that he gave him his own bed. But he did not ask. He might be new to Lonn's guard, but he already knew well enough not to question his prince.

"Assist me," Lonn eventually ordered, and Nife seemed glad to do so.

He activated more lamps, brightening the cozy tent and giving them enough light to work by. Together, they took off Llias' filthy shirt, cleaned his injuries and bandaged them. Ake's kit contained healing droughts and other potions and salves, but Lonn hesitated to use them. He remembered how his human friend David Thomen had reacted to a healing drought intended for an Otharnian, and he did not want Llias to experience any such problems. Lonn knew little of Fryst physiology, except that their skin and eye color was the result of living underground in their ice caves, far from the light of their sun. It would be risky to give Llias medicine intended for Otharnians, and so Lonn did not.

At some point before they finished with the bandages, Llias woke up. "...ere am I," he asked, fighting to sit up despite his slurred words and half-closed eyes.

"Llias, you are at my garrison," Lonn replied, his voice as gentle as the large hands finishing the bandages. He encouraged Llias to lie back down.

"Lonn. I 'member you," Llias muttered, resting back on the pillow, his eyes drifting closed again. Lonn smiled at him, pleased that the man had recalled his name, even if Llias didn't recall his title.

"If you can stay awake, something to eat will do you good," he said.

Llias forced his eyes open and Nife snatched up the cup of broth and held it out. Llias took it, but his hand shook as he tried to drink from it, enough that a few drops spilled on his bare chest. Lonn propped up the pillows behind him and steadied the cup as Llias slowly drank it, color coming back to his cheeks as he did. He was asleep again even as he drank the last drops, and Lonn laid him back down and covered him up. Nife took the cup, tidied up the tent and put Ake's healing kit back in order. It was hours before dawn, and it seemed that Prince Lonn was going to let this stranger sleep in his bed all night. Nife frowned to himself. "Shall I fetch a cot for your...guest, my prince?" he asked eventually, unsure what else to suggest.

Lonn shook his head, "No thank you, Nife," he said, pulling the chair over from the small desk and setting it next to the bed. "You should go and rest," he suggested, eager to be alone once more with Llias. Nife hesitated, the sight of Lonn sitting next to this Fryst man so unusual. It was not the first time the prince had guests in his bed, of course, but they usually were the kind that left before dawn with their pockets jingling. This was something new, and different.

"There is nothing more you need, my prince?" he asked, his brow furrowed. "Some food for yourself? Dry clothes? At least let me help you remove your armor..."

Lonn paused, Nife's solicitous questioning making him realize his wretched state. He was still in his leather and mail armor, the padded layers under it soaked through, and he had eaten nothing since midday. Lonn had been so focused on Llias that he had not even noticed. Even now, he was still tempted to send Nife away, so that he could bask in Llias' presence again, perhaps press his palm to his forehead and feel the strange bond trying to form between them. He shook himself. He would not do that. Not while Llias was unconscious, at least. "Yes," he forced himself to say, "Yes, of course."

It did not take long to get the armor off; Nife made short work of the straps and buckles, setting the pieces on the stand and briskly drying them off. He laid out fresh clothes for Lonn, and an extra set for Llias, then left to fetch some food.

Dry and comfortable, Lonn relaxed back in the chair, enjoying the quiet of the deep night. Llias was sleeping now, not the stillness of unconsciousness but true sleep, restful and healing. Lonn found himself breathing in time with him, his chest rising and falling in rhythm. He reached out his hand and brushed Llias' fingers. The Fryst man stirred, saw Lonn sitting there and mumbled something under his breath. Lonn could not be sure, but it sounded like his name.

Llias closed his eyes again, but he opened his hand and let Lonn intertwine his fingers. The bubbling thrill of arcane energy that rose there made Lonn's heart beat faster. The arcane connection was trying to grow, trying to bridge the distance between them. Lonn didn't react when Nife returned and set a plate by his side, and when he looked up later he was gone again.

Lonn luxuriated in the peace of the tent, the feel of Llias' hand in his. The small sounds of the nighttime garrison carried through the still air — the low murmur of voices, the occasional clink of armor, the crackle of early campfires. Lonn let it all wash over him, and sat with Llias as the stars turned above them

# Campfire

Lonn jerked awake when the sun was well up. His back ached from slumping on the chair next to the bed, and his mouth was sticky and dry. He stretched his arms above his head while something nagged at him, something that felt incomplete. When his eyes fell on the empty bed, he knew at once what it was.

Llias was gone.

Lonn leapt up and stormed out of the tent, his arcane senses flung wide, seeking his connection with Llias. He was furious and frantic, ready to punish whichever of his guards had let the man leave the camp without his permission. If any harm had come to him, Lonn would not be forgiving. He cared not what their excuse might be!

He was halfway through the camp when he heard a laugh and stopped short. Llias was sitting at the morning campfire with Ake, Nife and Myrun, another of the junior guards. Llias was wearing Lonn's spare clothes, eating breakfast and looking more recovered that Lonn would have thought possible. Lonn strode over to the cheerful group, where Llias was telling the tale of his adventure.

Ake saw Lonn approaching and jumped to his feet, the other guards following suit. Llias looked up last, standing when he saw who it was. Lonn's face must have betrayed his mood because Ake swiftly dismissed the two junior guards and faced the prince himself.

"Good morning, my prince," he said, setting his breakfast on the bench behind him, giving Lonn as little cause for anger as possible.

Ake was familiar with Lonn's temper, and was old and wise enough to let it wash over him without taking it personally. Lonn nodded at him, his blood still up from the sudden realization of Llias' absence. The Fryst man was looking at him curiously, his own breakfast plate still in his hand. Ake quickly rattled off his report of the company's return to camp the previous night, and the current status of the garrison and the companies, none of which Lonn listened to.

When he stopped talking, Lonn said, "Thank you, Lieutenant, you are dismissed."

Ake vanished, leaving Lonn and Llias alone. Lonn looked into Llias' face, for a moment falling into his eyes: deep, dark pools of midnight blue that seemed almost bottomless. The urge to reach out and touch Llias was almost irresistible, but Lonn held back. Instead, he took the plate of food and cup of *kurvorur* Nife silently brought him. The prince sat on the bench and gestured for Llias to sit as well, taking a sour but energizing sip from his hot drink. They sat for a moment, the fragrant smoke of the fire mingling with the smell of food in the chill morning air.

Llias did not wait for the prince to speak first; he drank from his own cup and said, "You are Prince Lonn of Otharn."

Lonn nodded. "Aye, I am," he replied.

Even as he sat in stillness, his arcane power pulsed with the beat of his heart, bubbling under his skin with the urge to escape its confinement, to be close to Llias. Cautiously, Lonn let a thread twine out from his chest — a slender and delicate thread, invisible even to himself. The thread drifted towards Llias, like a spider web in the summer breeze, and rested on his knee, as tender as a lover.

Llias shivered as though he had felt it and furrowed his brow, unsure what the sensation was. He shook it off, and continued, "I owe you my thanks, Prince Lonn, and I am happy to give it," he said. "Yesterday seems like a nightmare, but your guards tell me it was real. I don't know what that witch wanted to do with me, but I'm very glad she did not have a chance to do it. Thank you for getting me out of there."

"You are very welcome, Llias," Lonn said, his plate forgotten in his hands, the food uneaten. "You are feeling well?" he asked.

Llias nodded with a mouth full of bread. "Yes," he said, and held up his hand while he chewed and swallowed the food. "Yes," he said again, more distinctly, "I am well. I will be on my way and out of your hair soon enough, Prince Lonn."

The thread of Lonn's arcane power tightened around Llias' knee at that. Llias could not leave, but Lonn tried to be diplomatic.

"You are welcome to stay and recover your strength," he said, "The portal is still closed, and you will need to stay somewhere until it opens. This is Tornatt; the energy flow here only goes in one direction. Until it reverses, you will not be able to travel."

Llias rubbed his knee where Lonn's power had touched him in an unconscious gesture. "Thank you Prince Lonn, but I must not delay my return to Fryst. I am on the way to the temple, it will be midwinter soon, and I am needed. Your Lieutenant gave me directions to the nearest portal, and I will wait there. As soon as the portal opens, I will be ready."

Lonn scowled and tried again. Unused to resorting to persuasion, he was clumsy at it. It was far simpler to issue orders, but he had a feeling that approach would not work with this man.

"Llias," he said, "I ask you to stay another day. There is something about you that I do not yet understand. There is a connection between us. The witch took you for a reason, and I found you for a reason, although I do not know what it is."

"You said it was fate," Llias reminded Lonn with a frown.

"Maybe it was," the prince replied. "You feel it too, do you not?"

He pointed to Llias' knee, where the thread of power rested. Reaching over, he brushed his hand against Llias', letting his power rise, letting the threads spill over his fingers and fall into Llias' open palm. The connection was like fire, the threads hot and thrilling.

Llias' eyes widened, sparks from the campfire reflected there like stars. He stared at Lonn for a single, endless breath before he snatched his hand away.

"No," he said, shutting down the connection, pushing Lonn's magic away. Lonn was not sure if he did it consciously or if it was instinct, but the result was the same. The arcane threads were rejected, blown back as though a current had turned against them.

"No," Llias repeated, his hand a clenched fist, knuckles white against his blue fingers. "I don't feel anything. You are kind to offer to accommodate me, but I must be on my way."

He stood and Lonn stood with him, his anger growing. The lack of connection between them was as chill as winter where a moment ago it had been as hot as fire.

"What is so important that you will not give me one day?" Lonn demanded. "I saved your life. I bought you from that witch, carried you here and cared for you myself. Do you think you owe me nothing?"

Llias stepped back, the intensity of Lonn's reaction shocking him, rising out of nowhere. Lonn tried to control his temper, never an easy task at the best of times, but the damage was done. Llias was cold, his deep eyes narrowed, a purple flush on his pale blue cheeks.

"You *bought* me?" he said. "I am no slave, Lonn, and I owe you nothing except my thanks, which I have given." His voice was tight with emotion, "I cannot delay even one day. I am an *ishaxha*, I must bring light and warmth to the underground cities of Fryst. Already I am late, and my people will be waiting. I mean no offense, and I am grateful for what you have done, but I must go. My people need me."

"*I* need you," Lonn said, grabbing Llias' shoulder, trying to make him understand. "The connection is real, you cannot leave."

Llias wrenched his shoulder out of Lonn's grasp. "Excuse me, Prince Lonn," Llias said, his voice as icy as the air around him, "But you are mistaken. There is no connection between us, and I am leaving."

He turned his back on Lonn and walked away. Lonn stood by the fire, his jaw clenched, his breathing as slow and even as he could make it. He glanced around the camp and was not surprised to find that his guards had vanished from his sight. The woodpile was left half chopped, weapons went unsharpened, armor went unpolished. The very air seemed to hold its breath.

*Wise,* Lonn thought to himself, making an effort to unclench his jaw. His temper was known, and his patience had only lessened since the events of the past years had upended his family and taken his beloved brother away. If any other slave had spoken that way to him, Lonn had little doubt they would now be on their way to an unpleasant punishment. Lonn was not a cruel man, but he was a prince, and he carried that weight with him always.

"Captain," he said, his voice only a shade louder than usual. Hilde appeared, walking out from behind a tent as though she had just been passing by.

"Yes, my prince," she said, her tone level. She gave no indication at all that anything unusual had happened. She had seen nothing, and neither had anyone else.

Lonn pointed at Llias' disappearing figure. He was already past the prince's camp and heading for the edge of the garrison, brazenly disobeying Lonn's command. "Give my guest an escort," he ordered, "He is free to do as he pleases within the garrison and the hills. He will not go further than that."

Hilde nodded, "Yes, my prince," and hurried to carry out Lonn's instructions. Moments later, Nife and Myrun jogged out from the cook tent and set off after the Fryst man. Llias would not go back to Fryst. Not until Lonn gave him permission to do so.

# Spar

Disconnected threads of arcane energy surrounded Lonn as he sat by the campfire. He had a natural connection to the crystal realm, using its power through instinct more than training, and now his every instinct told him that it was wrong for Llias to leave. Lonn had never been as certain of anything in his life. Llias had not come to him through chance or luck, as the Fryst man had suggested, but through the designs of fate. They should be together.

Lonn ran his hands through his dark blond hair and let his awareness spread over the camp. The strands of energy surrounding him flowed as if in a strong current, and like a compass they pointed straight to Llias. Lonn was easily able to follow Llias' path as he walked the garrison perimeter and then headed up into the hills. Lonn's guards would be on his heels, and Lonn did not worry that Llias would get away from them. The Fryst man was unarmed and recently injured, whereas Lonn's guards were the elite of Otharnian troops. No, Llias was safe enough, but still Lonn's gut churned with discomfort at the distance between them.

He did not know how long he sat and brooded. It was not until a cheer rose from the central training area that he looked up. His back still ached from his uncomfortable night, and he was eager to let off some steam and loosen up his muscles. Inactivity did not suit him. He headed over to the training ring where he found Captain Rillen and his company conducting drills under their banner.

The training ring was in fact a square. The four companies of the garrison claimed a corner each with their banners. There was little to do while at camp except train, so Rillen and the other captains had organized regular contests between the companies. It had not taken long for wagers to follow. The most coveted prize was the right to hang the company banner over the best hot springs. The mountains behind the garrison had many such pools, but the losing companies had to trek high into the hills to bathe, while the winners enjoyed the steaming pools lower down. Rillen and his company had proudly hung their white *halfor* banner over the prized springs this round. From the way Rillen was haranguing his soldiers, Lonn could tell that he intended to keep it that way.

Lonn hailed the captain, his steps quickening at the sight of the soldiers. He knew what would help him throw off his discomfited mood and forget about Llias for a while.

"Spar with me," he demanded.

Rillen spun his wooden staff in his hand and nodded.

"Of course, my prince," he said, gesturing to a rack of staves and light armor ready for use.

Lonn stripped off his shirt and strapped banded-leather shielding to his guard-arm and shoulder. He saw his own guard behind him, who had followed him from his camp.

"Join us," he told the nearest one, Varla, who ducked under the wooden barrier and readied herself.

The damp ground was solid under Lonn's feet as he spun a staff in his hands and breathed out. Rillen and Varla faced off against him; behind them, the rest of Rillen's company ceased their training and arranged themselves to watch. Lonn ignored them, looking only at his opponents. Varla was lean and youthful where Rillen was heavier, older and wiser, but both were formidable fighters. Lonn was eager to face them. Already Llias and his disobedience were fading to the back of his mind. Only this moment mattered.

Lonn loved to fight. He loved the way his eye sharpened and focused on every tiny detail, every movement, every motion turned into a bolt of lightning from his brain to his body. It was not becoming of a prince, perhaps, but Lonn was what he was.

He waited for Rillen's nod, and when it came Lonn's strike swept the captain's feet out from under him, sending him tumbling backwards. Before the captain hit the ground, Lonn pivoted on the balls of his feet, the long arc of his staff turning with him, and sliced through the spot where Varla had stood a split second before. Lonn smiled. He would have to work for this victory. Neither of them would hold back out of respect for Lonn's rank, and Lonn would not hold back either. From the ground, Rillen's staff slammed into Lonn's knee, sending him stumbling into Varla's blow from above. Lonn dodged and returned the blow, his knee throbbing, his heart pounding, life pumping through his veins.

They fought, two against one, until they were covered in mud and sweat, Lonn's long hair tangled around his face, his guard-arm covered in bruises. Rillen had a cut above his eye, half-blinding him with blood, but he refused to yield, determined to give his prince the fight that he wanted.

Lonn feinted at Varla and the woman blocked, leaving her right side open for Lonn's real blow to slam into her ribs. But Lonn's weapon landed on air as Varla rolled, tossing her staff to her left hand and striking her own low blow, targeting Lonn's already injured knee. The hit landed and again Lonn stumbled. From behind, an enthusiastic cheer penetrated Lonn's consciousness.

He held up a hand to pause and turned to see Llias standing at the side of the ring, pointedly congratulating Varla for her hit. Nife and Myrun stood on either side of him, mortified, inching away so that Lonn would not associate them with Llias' obnoxious behavior.

Llias' presence was a warm, welcome glow, despite his provocation, and Lonn greeted him. "Llias," he said, his breath short from the exertion. "You enjoy the melee?"

Llias shrugged. "With the right competitors, I do," he said. "And if I must be your guest for another day, it seems only fair that you provide some entertainment, no?"

Despite himself, Lonn grinned at the man, ignoring the shocked faces of his guards. Lonn did not usually care for insolence, but this time he found he did not mind.

"Very well, then," he said, turning back to Rillen and Varla, ready to continue. If Llias wanted entertainment, Lonn would provide it.

"Although," Llias added, climbing over the wooden barrier and walking toward the competitors, "It looks as though Captain Rillen is already injured. You should swap him out, make it a fair fight."

Llias held out his hand for Rillen's staff, and Lonn choked as he realized Llias' intention. A shiver ran up his spine, and before he could think, he blurted out, "No."

Rillen froze, his arm outstretched in the act of giving his staff to Llias. Rillen had never known Lonn to refuse a challenge, and he had not expected him to do so now.

"No?" Llias said, his eyes narrowed, "You will not fight me?"

"You are injured," Lonn protested. He did not want to injure Llias more than he already was. Even if the Fryst man had some skill with a staff, he could not hope to compete with Lonn, who had been trained by the best of Otharn's weapon masters. However, Llias was showing no sign of his injuries; the truth was that the very idea of fighting Llias was somehow disturbing to Lonn. It felt wrong, and he did not want to do it.

"I am recovered," Llias insisted with a dark look, as though he knew there was more to Lonn's refusal.

Lonn shook his head, searching for some other reason but coming up with nothing other than, "*No.*"

Llias glared at Lonn, his voice a low hiss. "So, you will not let me leave, and you will not let me fight? What shall I do then, Lonn? Shall I return to your tent and await you in your bed?" Llias kept his voice down, but Rillen and Varla were close enough to hear his words. They exchanged an uncomfortable glance.

"No!" Lonn exclaimed.

He told himself that was not at all what he wanted, and shoved the thought out of his mind. Rillen's company were watching, silent and breathless. Lonn either had to let Llias fight, or the soldiers would have little doubt as to why Lonn kept him at his camp, and *that* was hardly going to persuade Llias to stay at the garrison any longer.

"At least wear some armor," Lonn finally conceded, pointing to the racks of armor and weapons.

With a triumphant smirk, Llias turned away.

# Protection

Lonn took the weight off his throbbing knee and leaned on his staff while Llias readied himself. Nife and Myrun jogged over to the weapon stands and helped Llias find a well-fitting leather chest plate and protection for his guard-arm.

The prince had no chest plate, but neither did he have recent injuries to that area, so he did not begrudge Llias one. Rillen offered his staff, but after some consideration Llias opted for the lighter *tanda* — dual-wielded sticks, each about the length of his arm. He flipped them in his hands, loose and comfortable, and strolled back out to Lonn.

"If I win, you will let me go," Llias declared loudly, spinning the sticks between his fingers, getting familiar with the weight and heft of them. The soldiers stirred with excitement at his challenge; now this might be a fight worth watching.

"You will not win," Lonn replied with a definitive shake of his head. He tossed his heavy staff and caught it, warming up his stiffening muscles. Lonn was at least half a head taller than Llias, his reach was longer, and he outweighed him. He had no doubts about who would win this match.

"Then promise me," Llias insisted with a wicked smile, his teeth gleaming white against his blue lips. "If your victory is certain, you have nothing to fear, no?"

The warmth coming off Llias was like a furnace, and Lonn's arcane power reached for it like a dog yearning for a place by the fire. Lonn could only hope Llias was as ignorant of it as he claimed, because short of letting him leave, Lonn suspected there was little else he could deny the man.

"Very well," he sighed, unable to refuse the challenge. "If you win, you are free to go. But you will not win."

Llias waved Varla to the side. She looked at Lonn, but he just shrugged and nodded. If Llias wanted to give away his advantage, Lonn would not stop him.

Llias flipped and caught his sticks one final time, then took his fighting stance. The *tanda* were well suited to Llias' lean frame, and he clearly knew how to use them. His form was excellent as he held the sticks steadily, one to attack and one to defend. Perhaps he would give Lonn more of a fight than the prince had expected, but Lonn took his own stance without concern. Their audience faded from Lonn's mind as he angled his staff to protect his weakened knee. Llias' keen eyes had no doubt already taken note of the weakness.

They paused for a beat, eyes locked, and Llias tapped his lead stick twice on the ground. *Was that some Fryst custom?* Lonn wondered; but before he could wonder any more, Llias attacked.

One of the *tanda* smashed into Lonn's guard-arm, hitting between the overlapping leather bands. It caught the point of his elbow and sent pain shooting up to his shoulder. Lonn's staff slipped from his numb fingers, and he had to block one-handed to stop Llias' other stick from taking his eye out. He almost dropped his staff from the force of the blow and stepped back, rapidly reassessing Llias' abilities. He was fast, and he was fearless.

Llias grinned at him, that captivating purple flush once again darkening his blue cheeks, delight flashing in his midnight eyes. "Surprised?" he asked. "The witch did not take me easily, you know."

"How *did* she take you?" Lonn asked, moving in a slow circle, looking for an opening in Llias' defense. He was intrigued as to how that weak-powered witch had managed to capture someone like Llias.

"Trickery," Llias spat with a sour look.

"I believe it," Lonn replied.

Even as he spoke, he surged forward and swung his staff at Llias' ribs. He did not use his full strength, but still the blow would have hurt if Llias had not dived under it and rolled. Llias flipped back to his feet and jabbed one of his sticks into Lonn's tender knee, turning his balance. The prince quickly found himself facing the wrong way with his weight on the wrong leg. Llias followed up with another swift strike, which Lonn managed to catch on his armored shoulder. He forgot the second stick, though, and Llias rapped his knuckles to remind him, dancing back on light feet, the curl of a satisfied smile on his lips.

"Shall I ask Nife to pack my things?" he asked, clearly mocking the prince, as he had no things to pack. Even the clothes he wore were Lonn's.

Lonn scowled. He was done with this game. His eyes narrowed and he shook off the throbbing of his bruises; he would attend to that later. He watched Llias move. The man was good at hiding it, but his wounds were still tender. He turned the injured side away from Lonn, putting himself off balance.

A quick feint towards that side forced Llias to move to protect himself. Quick as lightening, Lonn reversed his grip and gave Llias' wrist a blow that sent one of his sticks flying. Lonn pressed his advantage, sweeping Llias' feet and forcing him to scramble back, his remaining stick held in both hands at guard position.

Usually Lonn's arcane power was nothing but an afterthought unless he was actively seeking it. But as soon as Lonn's staff connected with Llias' wrist, it had surged to life. Now it swirled all around him, frantic at the battle. He swatted the magic away, but like a stirred fire it burst back, twisting around Lonn's legs and slowing him down, making him stumble as he pursued Llias to finish the fight.

Lonn growled and focused, forcing his magic back, bottling it up and trying to ignore it. His vision narrowed, darkening at the edges as he followed Llias with long strides, his staff at the ready. Llias would not be leaving the garrison; Lonn needed to end this battle and end all doubt. He swung his staff at Llias' belly, a brutal blow that sent him staggering back, gasping for air, the breath forced out of him. The ground shuddered and Lonn fell to one knee. He ignored the unexpected fall, lurching back to his feet and pursuing his prize once more.

"Yield!" he demanded, sending Llias to the ground with another blow.

Llias rolled and flipped back to his feet, his stick striking Lonn's elbow again, a blow the prince hardly felt. Why would the man not stay down?

Rocks tumbled from the nearby hills, and Lonn staggered as the ground cracked under his feet. Llias was yelling at him now, words that Lonn couldn't hear through the pounding in his ears.

The threads of arcane power whipped at Lonn, tangling his arm and trying to pry his fingers from his staff. He would not let it go. Not until Llias had yielded to him. The staff creaked as his magic flared and smashed to splinters in his hand, shards of wood burrowing into his flesh like knives.

His arcane power was wild now, burning through his body, a force that he had never felt before. For the first time in his life, the power felt like an adversary, like an untamed beast instead of a loyal hound. Lonn fell to the ground; from the other side of the arena his soldiers ran towards him, but they were too far away. Lonn tasted blood, his back arched, his bones creaking. The power flooding his body was too much for him to contain. His body could not hold it; it was fighting to escape him, and he could not summon Skarpur to channel it. Lonn had lost control, and there was nothing he could do to help himself.

Llias threw down his *tanda* and crashed into him, shoving him down on his back. Warm blue hands pressed on his bare chest, burning his skin, and finally Lonn could hear Llias' voice: "...focus, focus you idiot, I'm trying to help you..."

Like a rampaging torrent swirling through a sinkhole into deep darkness, Lonn's arcane power drained away, falling into the bottomless well of Llias' soul. Lonn gasped. The sudden flow of magic was like the draw of a silk feather over his every nerve. A still, silent moment rang between them like a bell, clear and bright, and his eyes met Llias', bright blue staring into midnight velvet. Neither of them breathed.

The moment was brief, then sound returned to the world with a pop, the ground settled under Lonn's body, and the world stilled its wild dance. The camp and the surrounding garrison was silent. Only Llias, sitting on Lonn's thighs, made a sound. He leaned down and spoke into Lonn's ear. "I think that is my victory."

Lonn coughed, his mouth full of dust and blood. His entire body ached. His head was pounding like the worst hangover he had ever had. His knee was a ball of throbbing pain. A hundred cuts and splinters from his disintegrated staff made themselves known. Despite that, and despite being flat on his back on the muddy ground, thoroughly undignified, Lonn managed to say, "You threw down your weapon. That means I won."

He stared up at the sky as Llias scowled and climbed off him, the sudden lack of contact making his pains so much worse. The flames of Lonn's arcane power were already re-emerging, reaching out for Llias, folding protectively around him. Lonn had a sinking feeling about what that meant, and he didn't dare mention it. He could only hope that Llias had not worked it out for himself.

Lonn climbed to his feet and looked around. The ground was churned up as though a team of oxen had come through with a heavy plow; lines and fissures radiated out from where he stood. The soldiers stared at him, open-mouthed. Even Rillen was struck dumb.

"Want to get out of here?" Llias muttered under his breath. Lonn had never wanted anything more. He did not care for the looks of disbelief and shock from his soldiers. Lonn glared at Rillen, as though daring him to speak, but he did not.

"Llias and I are going to the springs," Lonn announced. "Captain, please take care of this—"

Lonn waved a hand at the training arena, the torn-up ground, the destroyed weapons racks, the shards of Lonn's former spear embedded in the dirt like a thousand newly planted thorns. He searched for the right word, but all he could come up with was: "—this *mess*."

Rillen nodded, then seemed to finally remember his words. "Yes, my prince," he said.

He turned and ordered his company to start cleaning up, shaking off his shock and getting his soldiers to do the same. Lonn beckoned to Llias, and they turned in the other direction. Lonn leaned on Llias' shoulder, and Llias snatched the healing kit Ake wordlessly held out to him as they passed.

# Hot-Spring

"All right, so perhaps we do have a connection," Llias said as he led Lonn up the steep path behind the garrison to the hot springs.

"I told you," Lonn grumbled, leaning on Llias as the gravel rolled under his feet, wrenching his injured knee. "You should have listened."

"*You* should control yourself!" Llias retorted, unimpressed.

He turned down the narrow path that led to the pool Lonn's guard had claimed for themselves. It was not as large or deep as the most prized locations, but Lonn and his guard had fewer people to share it with, and it was the closest to the garrison. The sun was past its peak, but the shelter of the cliffs trapped what heat there was, forming a warm, rocky bowl leading to the steaming pool. Lonn didn't go there much, preferring to leave his guard to relax without his presence looming over them, but now it was deserted.

"Nife and Myrun showed me this place earlier today," Llias said, "It reminds me of home. There are hot springs under the ice of Fryst a hundred times the size of this one."

Lonn kicked off his boots and sank into the pool, still half-dressed, the warm water easing his battered body and soothing his aching knee. He let out a long sigh and tried to unbuckle the armor from his guard-arm.

Llias took off his borrowed armor and clothes and climbed into the pool in his underwear. His side was no longer bandaged, and the cut that had been deep and bloody the day before was now merely tender and swollen. He healed fast.

"Idiot," he said to Lonn, "You have got the straps wet."

Sitting on the rocky ledge next to the prince, he wrestled with Lonn's armor fastenings until they came away. Lonn sighed and sank into the water, ducking under and floating there. His nerves were still singing at the memory of Llias' touch, at the thrill of him draining the arcane power from his body.

When he emerged, Llias had Ake's healing kit laid out by the side of the pool. He held up a pair of tweezers. "I will pull out your splinters if you admit I won that fight," he offered.

"Why would I admit something that is not true?" Lonn asked, "You threw down your weapon."

"You disintegrated *your* weapon first," Llias snapped back.

That was true, and Lonn grunted his acceptance. "A draw, then," he said, and took the tweezers from Llias' hand to work on his own arm. He was using his wrong hand, and his knuckles were still swollen from the hit Llias had landed on it earlier. It was slow progress, and evidently Llias was too impatient to watch him fumble.

"Come here," he said with a roll of his eyes, gesturing for the tweezers back.

Lonn obediently returned them and let Llias start the slow, painstaking job of pulling out the dozens of splinters in his flesh.

"If I had kept my weapon, your own magic would have strangled you," Llias observed, in a reasonable tone.

"You felt it, then," Lonn said, pushing his dripping hair out of his face.

Llias gave him a dark look and yanked out a large splinter. "Everyone felt it, Lonn! You let your power get out of control. You could have been seriously hurt, or worse, if I hadn't stopped you. Does that happen often?"

Drops of water scattered from Lonn's hair as he shook his head. Llias turned his arm over, looking for more splinters. Lonn flinched as he found one. Perhaps Llias was merely looking for more opportunities to jab Lonn with the sharp tweezers.

"It has never happened before," he admitted, and it was true. He had never come close to losing control like that.

Skarpur could hold vast stores of power, and even in battle Lonn was in control of his channeling, firing sizzling bolts of energy from his spear or sending energy to his brother to use in his more refined castings. Vell had always told him to spend more time learning to harness his powers, but he had never listened. And now this had happened. Lonn let his head fall back and duck under the water again, hoping to wash away the shame of it.

"You see why I want you to stay," he said when he emerged.

Satisfied that he had got all the visible splinters out, Llias tossed the tweezers down. "If it never happened before, Lonn, you should let me go far, far away from you so it doesn't happen again!" he said, frustrated. "You could have died, and I doubt your loyal soldiers would have thought too hard about who to blame for it."

He jerked a thumb at himself and pushed off from the ledge, swimming to the opposite side. It was only a dozen feet away, but Lonn could feel the distance as his magic followed Llias like a forlorn puppy.

"It felt good, when you touched me," Lonn confessed. "Did you feel that too? It felt like...it felt like you were touching my magic, all the way through me. It felt...intimate."

Llias glanced away, a slight blush on his cheeks that could perhaps be attributed to the warm water. Or perhaps not.

Lonn tried his luck. "Come back over here," he said, beckoning. "Come sit on my lap and let us see if it happens again."

Surprised, Llias let out a snort of laughter. He found a stone on the rocky edge of the pool and tossed it at Lonn's head — a slow, lazy throw that had little force behind it. Lonn's hand snapped up and he caught the stone with a hopeful smile.

"Absolutely not!" Llias said, but his eyes crinkled. "You can forget about that, Lonn. I have this little rule, you see — no lap-sitting for anyone who's keeping me prisoner."

"You're not a prisoner, Llias. I would like you to stay as my guest."

"A guest who can leave whenever he wants?" Llias asked, his nose wrinkled, "Or a guest who's not allowed to leave, which, by the way, is also known as a *prisoner*."

Lonn had no reply, because they both knew the answer. Despite that, the tension between them drained away as Lonn's raging power had.

Llias splashed water on his face, the heat of it drawing purple highlights to his blue cheeks, his hair black with the weight of the water. "Did the witch do this to us?" he asked, "Is this connection her doing?"

Lonn shook his head. "I don't think so," he said, thinking as he spoke. "This doesn't feel like something malevolent. It feels good, it feels right." A hungry shiver ran up his spine at the memory, and he tried to focus. "Perhaps she sensed it, and used you to bait a trap for me."

"What kind of trap?" Llias asked, swimming out to the middle of the pool and treading water there, closer to Lonn but still not close enough for them to touch. "I don't remember much, but you made an oath to her, didn't you? What was it?"

Lonn groaned, his foolishness about to become apparent. "I do not know," he admitted, his arm aching where the oath-magic had bound him. "It was an oath to perform a favor for her, upon her request."

"And you agreed to that?" Llias exclaimed, incredulous.

"I had to!" Lonn snapped back, "She would have let you die in her cage if I had not. Think me a fool if you must, but I could not let that happen!"

"Well, I suppose I cannot disapprove of your reasoning." Llias said, deigning to swim a little closer, "But we still have a problem, Lonn: I need to leave, and you want me to stay. And as you are the crown prince and commander of these soldiers that surround us, you are entirely capable of enforcing your wishes. Still, surely you know I won't explore this bond with you under such conditions. I won't, and you'll gain nothing except my resentment by keeping me here against my will."

Lonn kicked off from the ledge and swam out to meet Llias, the fading sunlight sparkling on the water around them.

"I will send resources to Fryst," he offered. "You said you bring light and warmth to your people in their underground cities. I can do that. Food too. Whatever is needed I can do, Llias. I am the crown prince and I can order it so. Your people will not suffer if you stay."

"Hmph," Llias said, but he did not swim away, and Lonn pressed his advantage.

"It will be well for Fryst, will it not, to have such an agreement with Otharn? Tribute usually goes the other way, but I will arrange it. You can work for your people by staying with me."

"You would have me sell myself? To give up my life as *ishaxha* and become what? Your...your *companion*? I will not sit on your lap, Lonn, no matter how much tribute you send to Fryst."

Lonn tentatively held out his hand, letting himself float in the water within reach of Llias. "I do not know what name to give it, and you do not have to do anything you do not want to."

"Except stay," Llias said, letting his own fingers brush against Lonn's.

The tingling rise of magic bubbled through the prince's blood. "Yes," Lonn said. "Except that. Stay with me."

Llias snatched his hand away, cutting the connection again. He swam to the edge of the pool. "I will think it over," he said shortly, and climbed out, picking up his discarded clothes.

Lonn nodded. "Very well," he said, enjoying the warm water too much to leave it yet. He would give Llias some time to think about his decision. "You are returning to the garrison?"

At Llias' nod, Lonn called out, "Guard!"

Nife appeared at the head of the path. Hilde trained her company well, and Lonn had known there would be guards nearby, even close to the camp.

Llias scowled. "I do not need a babysitter."

"Perhaps not," Lonn said, "But you do need an escort. My companies are on Tornatt because of raiders, and even here we cannot be too careful. You do not even have a weapon."

Llias made the same motion he had made in the Varhin market, a hand reaching over his shoulder and finding nothing there.

"Give me one, then," he said, and Lonn saw no reason to deny him. Everyone had the right to defend themselves, after all, and a gesture of goodwill to Llias would not go amiss.

"You can have the *tanda*, if you want," he offered. "You fought well with them."

"I *won* with them," Llias retorted. "And I will take them, thank you. I would like a bow as well, if you can spare one."

Lonn nodded, "Of course," he said, amused at Llias' demand. He might call himself a prisoner, but he had no qualms about asking his jailer for favors.

"Nife will help you find one tomorrow." Lonn added, looking over at his guard. Nife nodded, and with that Llias pulled on his clothes and left, the crunch of feet on gravel fading in the distance.

# Price

Lonn swam back and forth in the pool for a long time, letting the warm water wash past him until his muscles burned and his mind emptied. Only then did he let himself float, and he was surprised to see stars overhead, twinkling through the mist that rose from the water. The fireflies were out too, casting their green glow around the rocky bowl of the spring.

It was quiet, the bubble of water over the rocks the only sound. Lonn drifted, feeling strangely peaceful. He had made his offer to Llias, and he would await his decision. He was hopeful that Llias would decide correctly, but even if that did not happen, Lonn would not give up. He could be persuasive when he wanted to be. He had both reward and punishment at his command, and although he preferred not to use the latter, he would if he had to.

A shadow caught his eye, looming in the mist, and Lonn grabbed the rocky edge of the pool, alarmed.

"Who goes there?" he demanded, squinting through the damp air. A figure stepped forward, mist melting away to reveal the tall, hooded witch from the Varhin.

"You!" Lonn said, leaping out of the water on the opposite bank and summoning Skarpur to his hand.

"Peace, Prince," the witch said with a smirk in her tone. "You will not need that. We have a bargain, you and I."

She held up her hand, the robe falling back to reveal the oath-magic glittering on her burned fingers. Lonn looked down to see the same on his own hand. The magic had sunk bone-deep.

"What do you want?" Lonn demanded, uneasy that the woman knew who he was.

She laughed and tossed her head. The gesture triggered a twinge of familiarity, but Lonn could not place where he had seen it before.

"You are happy with your purchase?" the witch asked, amused at some joke Lonn was not party to. "You have seen what he can do for you, and your union will only deepen. He is an asset for a warrior-prince such as yourself. Now that your magic has found its familiar, you will never be satisfied without him."

"My what?" Lonn snapped. He shook his head, confused. "My familiar?"

The witch laughed again, cold and mocking. "You did not realize? That is what he is: your arcane familiar, the heart of your power. Did you learn nothing from your magic tutors, Prince? With him, your power will grow beyond your imagining. You will rival your father before long. You have me to thank for that, and thank me you will."

"What do you want?" Lonn asked, his fist tight around Skarpur, his temper rising. He refused to engage in banter with the sinister woman.

Still she evaded his question, tossing her head again and wriggling under her robe as though eager to shake it off. "You promised me a favor, Prince, and if you break your oath, I will take back your familiar and you will be powerless to stop me. He carries my hunter's mark, and I will always find him. If you do not give me the favor you owe me, he will die — and I will make sure he knows it is because you are an oath breaker."

"Name your price then, witch!" Lonn yelled, his heart pounding in his ears at the idea of losing Llias so soon after finding him. It was intolerable.

"Witch?" the woman hissed. "Many have called me that, and all have regretted it, Prince."

She tossed her head again and Lonn's unease rose, the feeling of familiarity growing.

"Who are you?" he whispered, his arcane power rising again, unbidden.

The length of Skarpur's blade crackled with it. Lonn forced it back, banking it like a fire. Llias' voice echoed in his ears: *You should control yourself.* Llias was not there to help him now, if Lonn should let it overcome him once more.

On the other side of the pool, half-hidden by mist, the woman flung back her hood, showing her face to the stars and the fireflies. Not only her arm was burned, but her head too — mottled red and weeping, her scalp patchy with raw skin and the remnants of blond hair. "Do you know me now, Prince?" she asked.

Lonn staggered back, horrified.

"Lady Illt?" he croaked, the realization slamming into him as he finally recognized the formerly doll-like sorcerer who had been his father's hidden left hand. "What has happened?" he demanded, cold fear twisting in his gut, "Why are you here?"

Illt stepped out over the pool, her feet bending the surface tension of the water but not breaking it. The hem of her robe floated, as dry as it had been on the rocky ground. Lonn clenched his jaw at her casual display of power. He had thought her some pitiful hedge-witch and not the powerful sorcerer he knew her to be. He cursed himself and stood firm as she approached, Skarpur still at the ready by his side.

Illt faced Lonn, eye to eye. She was the same height as he, and she forced him to look directly at her, at the burned flesh twisting her mouth, one eye half-closed, the other bloodshot and watering.

"What happened? Your cursed elskan brother did this to me! He and his owner, that ridiculous human!"

"Do not speak of Vell in that manner," Lonn spat. "Tell me what has become of him!"

He grabbed Illt's shoulder. A repulsion spell flung him back across the ground — nothing like the weak little thing she had cast in the Varhin. Lonn landed on his feet though, too well trained to let go of Skarpur in the face of an attack. The blade flared with magic, dark shadows writhing like ink behind Illt's still form.

Illt's mocking laugh floated through the mist. "I will speak of him as he deserves. His master has put him to use and planted another monster in his belly, a creature of fur and fangs, another threat to the joined worlds that will be born from his unnatural lust."

Lonn's head swam, and his jaw ached from clenching it. *Not again,* he thought. Everything that had befallen his brother after his first disastrous pregnancy resurfaced at once: Vell's flight from Otharn, his crimes on Earth, his capture and punishment. It had taken Lonn years to get his brother back to safety after that. *Not again.*

Illt's laugh was colder this time. "Your father tried to deal with him, but the old man has grown sentimental and refused to strike him down when he had the chance. He underestimated them both. He allowed them to slip through his fingers and cast the blame for his failure on me!"

The witch rolled her head, her bones cracking like firewood. "I lost my mages in battle with those two and they were almost my end as well. Every protective artifact I had is nothing but ash. The human has some power I have never seen before, and he has trained Vell to channel it for him. They escaped from Otharn, and the king bid me leave as well."

"He banished you?" Lonn asked, startled. He had no love for Illt or her methods, but she had always seemed loyal to the king. Banishment was a harsh punishment indeed for a single failure, especially one that had come at such a cost, and for someone the king had found so useful as Lady Illt.

"He did," Illt confirmed, a world of fury contained in her tone. "My every sacrifice in his service was dismissed and so was I, because of your brother's *monsters*. He and his master think me dead; they think themselves safe with their spawn, but they are not! They did not defeat me, and they will pay the price."

Lonn gripped Skarpur with iron fingers. Horror was clawing its way up his throat and the oath magic burned on his arm. He knew what Illt was going to say, and he had no way to stop her.

"The children," she said.

The prince's blood chilled as her burned mouth twisted into an ugly smile.

"The monster that grows in your brother's belly and the monster that walks the worlds. That is my price for the Fryst slave. That is the favor I would have from you, Prince. Bring me those ill-gotten babes alive, and your oath will be fulfilled. Fail me, and I will take your familiar instead. Tell no one of this bargain."

Before Lonn could say another word, Illt faded into the shadows. Lonn yelled for his guard, and Nife ran down the rocky pathway, his weapon in hand. Together they searched the spring and the surrounding cliffs, but Lonn was not surprised to find nothing.

"Where is Llias?" Lonn asked as they strode back down the rocky pathway to the garrison.

"Your guest is sleeping, my prince," Nife said, slightly out of breath from accompanying Lonn's long stride. "I gave him my cot in the guard's tent. I hope that is acceptable?"

Nife's young face was anxious, unsure of the status of this guest. Was a narrow cot in the guard's tent too meagre accommodation for him, or was it too generous? Llias was a mystery to the guards, and Lonn's strange regard for him even more so.

The first thing Lonn did when they returned was to check the tent. Llias indeed slept there, beneath a blanket on a narrow bed between Myrun and Varla. He nodded.

"That is fine, Nife. Fetch Captain Hilde?"

Nife jogged off to find Hilde, and Lonn paced the open area by the fire pit, his feet making anxious trails in the dirt while he waited.

Only a few minutes later, Hilde arrived with Captain Rillen, their clothes in hasty disarray. Lonn looked them over and dismissed the observation from his mind. He had little care how his captains spent their free time.

"Prince Lonn," she said, breathless from running across the garrison. She looked at him, at his muddy feet and bared spear, his soaked clothes and wild eyes. "What happened?" she asked, her hand on the hilt of her sword.

Lonn pointed up into the hills with Skarpur. "The witch."

There was no need to say anything else.

"I'll take my company and search the hills," Rillen said. "If she's there, we'll find her." Obviously, whatever else they had been doing, Hilde had taken then time to brief her fellow captain on the strange circumstances surrounding Llias' purchase and arrival at the garrison.

"Wait," Lonn said. "Before you go, know this. It is no mere hedge-witch that we are dealing with. She is Lady Illt of Otharn, a most powerful and dangerous sorcerer."

"Lady Illt?" Hilde said, her eyes wide.

She was better acquainted with the king's sorcerer than Rillen, and she knew how formidable an adversary Illt could be. When they were all younger, Lonn and his guard had enjoyed sparring with Illt, pitting her magic against the guards' strength and Lonn's enchanted spear. Their bouts had grown increasingly brutal, and one day Vell had returned from a trip to the forest and told them to stop. Illt was too dangerous, he had warned. If they continued to spar with her, they would be giving away information that she could use against them. Hilde had ended the sparring matches over Lonn's objections, but soon enough even Lonn saw the sense of Vell's warning. Illt had started hunting and slaying magical creatures in dark rituals, adding to her power, growing more twisted and less controlled as the years passed.

"Take great care," Hilde warned Rillen with a shiver. "Do not separate your troops; no groups of less than six."

Rillen nodded and headed to his camp to rouse his soldiers.

Lonn turned to Hilde. "She has called in her favor," he said, but before he could say more his tongue stilled in his mouth. He could not speak it.

"What did she want?" Hilde asked, her hand on her sword hilt.

Lonn could not speak. His arm ached where the oath-magic bound him, pain shooting down to the bone. A warning.

Hilde stared at him, confused. "My prince?"

Lonn tried to force himself to speak, but to no avail. He lowered Skarpur and grabbed his wrist, seeking to ease the ache.

Hilde frowned, her eyes on the spot Lonn cradled.

"The oath," she said slowly, and Lonn nodded.

Lady Illt had told him to tell no one of her demand, and the oath was enforcing her will. It would not allow him to reveal her price.

"My prince," Hilde said, concerned, "Perhaps it would be wise to return to Otharn. Your father may be able to assist with this matter."

Lonn's jaw ached from grinding his teeth. He had had no choice but to make the oath to save Llias' life, but Lonn had no way to fulfill Illt's demand. It was impossible for him to hunt his own brother and hand over his children to the witch, for whatever foul purpose she had. Even if she wanted nothing more than to earn the king's forgiveness, it would still end with the death of the children, and that was something Lonn would not do. And now he could not even talk about it with his captain!

In a fit of temper and frustration, Lonn drew back his arm and threw Skarpur over the camp. The weapon trained golden sparks as it flew like a comet and disappeared.

Hilde watched it fly, her face tight with worry. Lonn turned away and stomped to his tent to wait for the sun.

# Orange Blossom Underground

Llias woke early to the whispers of Myrun and Varla in the guards' tent. Eavesdropping was impolite, but so was keeping innocent people prisoner; Llias didn't trouble too much about his manners as he lay perfectly still and listened.

*"...he says he's a guest, but we all know what that means."*

That was Myrun's voice. Llias had made a note of the guards' names and faces, and he knew Myrun from his first morning at the campfire. She enjoyed gossip a little too much for a prince's guard, and Llias thought she might be useful.

*"You should watch your tongue."*

That was Varla's short tone. Llias hadn't spoken to her properly yet, but she eyed him suspiciously and hadn't responded to his attempts to strike up a conversation with her. Still, she had tossed him a blanket last night when Nife had shown him the narrow cot he could sleep on. Llias knew enough to be grateful for that small kindness.

The soft sounds of the two women pulling on their uniforms and boots had almost lulled Llias back to sleep when Myrun whispered again, *"He slept in the prince's bed last night. Nife told me."*

*Ah,* Llias thought. So young Nife was a gossip too, or perhaps he was just naïve enough to let Myrun probe him for information. Another useful tidbit.

"It's none of your concern who the prince has in his bed," Varla muttered. A moment later, she relented and added, "Although I can see why he'd be tempted with this one."

That sounded like his cue, so Llias opened his eyes, startling the two women staring down at him appraisingly. He gave them a winning smile, no trace of anything he had overheard showing on his face.

"Good morning, ladies," he said, sitting up and stretching his back.

Myrun almost fell over her feet in her hurry to leave the tent, but Varla stayed and finished fastening her boots.

"Nife is expecting you at the training ground," she said. "I'll escort you."

Llias nodded. He already knew where the training ground was, of course. He had made a careful circuit of the entire garrison camp the day before, noting all the important locations and the distance and direction between them. The camp was too open for his liking. The sky was too high above them, and there were no protective walls, no passageways with twists and turns to memorize. It was just one big, open space, with tents and roped-off areas scattered like the spokes of a wheel. It was laughably easy to memorize the layout, and Llias had done it with Lonn's guards dogging his steps, thinking he was sulking at his ill luck.

"Thank you, Varla," he said with another easy smile.

Varla let her eyebrows rise a fraction, surprised and perhaps suspicious that Llias knew her name. She nodded and turned to leave, then looked back. "You can eat with us, if you hurry up."

The offer of food was too good to pass up, so Llias rolled out of his uncomfortable bed and followed Varla to the cook tent. He was given the same breakfast as the guards: a bowl of porridge and a cup of the sour *kurvorur* the Otharnians loved. He drank it and tried not to make a face; it really was horrible stuff. Seeing a stack of freshly baked bread rolls, he grabbed one to eat on the way. Varla and Ake fell in behind him as he left the cook tent and headed to the training ground.

A scent on the breeze caught his attention, and before he could stop himself, he had halted in the path. Lonn's tent was close by, and Llias knew, despite what his senses told him, that there was no scent coming from that direction.

Llias had smelled orange blossom once before, when he had visited the secret oasis of Nadige to be initiated as *ishaxha*. The priests were rightfully proud of their orange trees, carefully cultivated for hundreds of years underground in simulated crystal light and warmed by the heat of the volcanic springs. The smell of the blossom seeped back into Llias' mind now, as he stared at the spot where the prince slept.

When he had first seen those orange trees and smelled their intoxicating scent, Llias had wanted to seize hold of them and press his face into the blooms. He had wanted to inhale them into his lungs, to consume them and make them a part of himself. He had the same urge now, an almost physical desire to do the same with Lonn's stupid, handsome face. Llias breathed in deeply, but not a worldly scent this time. No pollen floated on the light breeze to tempt him closer; it was something deeper, more primal than that. It was something he had not known was missing from his life until he had experienced it, just like those captivating trees with their pale blossoms. He had never forgotten the smell of orange blossom; he had dreamed about it on and off for years since leaving Nadige. He breathed in again, tasting nothing on the air. Despite that, his mouth watered, hungry although he had just eaten.

Llias lacked the words to describe it, but he did not lack the will to resist it. Orange blossom or not, stupid, handsome face or not, Llias could resist. He was an *ishaxha* of Fryst, and he was needed there, not here.

Lonn had promised him a weapon, and Llias was not so foolish as to give the prince time to change his mind. If he was going to escape, he needed to be armed.

He turned his back on Lonn's tent and on the heavy scent that lingered in his mind, and headed to the training ground.

# Bow

Lonn opened his eyes the next morning and at once he knew the flow of energy around Tornatt had reversed. It was as clear to his arcane senses as the direction of the tide was to someone with eyes. He stared up at the canvas ceiling of his tent. The timing of this reversal could not be more suspicious, but no force Lonn knew of could change the direction of the energy flow, not even his own father. It must be nothing but coincidence that it had happened the very day after Illt made her demands.

But nevertheless, Lonn was glad of it; it was past time for him to return home. Even a few hours of rest had refreshed him and cleared the confusion from his mind. He would return to Otharn and find out what had happened to his brother, and he would take Llias with him, keeping him safe in the palace, far from Illt's grasp. It was the logical thing to do, and his heart lightened at his decision. He only had to inform Llias they would be leaving.

He checked the guards' tent and was not surprised to find Llias gone. The guards were early risers, and Llias would have hardly been able to sleep in. He was not at the campfire either, but Hilde was waiting for her commander there.

"Rillen's company searched the hills and found nothing, my prince. Llias is at the training grounds." She answered his unspoken questions as she handed him a cup of hot *kurvorur* and a plate. "Nife said you ordered him to find Llias a weapon this morning?"

She made the statement sound like a question, and Lonn did not blame her. He was arming a man he had only met the day before, the same man he had bought in exchange for an unbreakable oath to a witch; the same man he had been unable to defeat in the ring, although he had defeated dozens of opponents stronger and faster than him. Hilde would not be doing her job if she did not ask, but Lonn had no way to explain.

"I did," he said instead, and beckoned her to follow him as he headed to the training grounds, eating as he walked.

He was conscious that he was trailing after Llias like a pup after its master, but he could not stop. The tug of his arcane power urged him on, making him eager to see the Fryst man again, to be close to him. He did his best to slow his steps, to seem calm and controlled, but he did not know if he'd succeeded.

Hilde had obviously been waiting for him for a reason other than to give him breakfast, and Lonn waited for her questions.

"My prince," she began, "Who is Llias? Is he an agent of that witch? Does he have some power over you? You do not want him to leave, but we can keep him securely. You do not have to arm him and let him roam as he pleases."

Lonn sighed and handed his empty cup and plate to a passing page. "Captain," he said, "there is more afoot than I can explain, but Llias is no danger to me, I can assure you of that. You do not need to throw him in the stockade."

Hilde's dark look suggested she wanted to do that exact thing, and Lonn clapped her on the shoulder, warmed by her loyalty. She had known him since he was young, and had been one of his personal guards before she became captain. Hilde had had the chance to move on from that role and rejoin the main army, where she would have risen in the ranks, but she never had. They walked on, side by side.

Llias and Nife were at the training ground. They had set up targets, and Llias was trying out the selection of bows that Nife had dug up. Lonn paused to watch. Llias was still wearing Lonn's borrowed clothes, the cuffs of the trousers turned up a few inches, the left sleeve of the shirt rolled up over his elbow and a leather bracer around his forearm. He had a quiver of arrows over his shoulder, and Lonn finally understood the reaching gesture he had made at the market and at the spring. Llias was an archer. A good one, by the look of the arrows buried in the centers of the targets. He pulled back the string and paused, the light breeze ruffling his dark blue hair. Lonn held his breath at the sight as the morning sun behind Llias silhouetted his precise form; hips, elbow, wrist, and arrow were all perfectly aligned with the target. The breeze dropped, and Lonn breathed again as the arrow *thunked* into the center of the next target.

Lonn swallowed. His earlier suggestion for Llias to come sit on his lap had been made mostly in jest, but now Lonn was strongly reconsidering the seriousness of the offer. The man really did have excellent form. As though reading his thoughts, Llias turned and saw him standing there, staring. Despite himself, Lonn blushed. Llias gave him a knowing look and the thread of arcane power between them lurched as though Llias had pulled on it. Lonn lurched half a step forward before he got control of his feet.

Nife and Hilde looked at each other, confused, and Lonn realized the silence had lingered too long.

"Good morning, Llias," he forced himself to say. "I am glad to see you have found a weapon that suits you."

Llias nodded his thanks to the young guard who stood beside him. "Nife has been patient with me," he said, "I prefer a straight bow, but this one is close enough."

Lonn examined Llias' choice of bow. It was a recurve, as all Otharnian bows were, to deliver more power with the same draw length.

"A straight bow is not as powerful," he said, handing it back for Llias to holster it over his shoulder in the quiver Nife had found him. Lonn noted that he had the *tanda* sticks tucked into the same quiver. Practical.

"A straight bow is quieter, though," Llias said, collecting his arrows from the target. "Sound carries in the ice-caves, and I don't like too much attention."

There was no avoiding it any longer. Llias was looking at Lonn, curious as to his purpose here. It would not win him any of Llias' regard, but Lonn could not let him stay here on Tornatt, even in the garrison, with Illt on the loose. Her threat to take Llias back and kill him if Lonn did not comply with her impossible demand echoed in Lonn's head, and he could not shake it off. He was hopeful that Llias had considered his offer of tribute to Fryst. It was a good offer, and Lonn could not see why he would refuse.

"Llias, I am returning to Otharn, and you will accompany me."

Even as he said it, Lonn knew he had phrased it badly. He was used to issuing orders to soldiers and subordinates, not trying to persuade willful out-worlders to accept his indefinite and compulsory hospitality.

Llias raised his eyebrows and folded his arms. "I would rather not, Lonn," he said shortly. The link between them, warm and friendly a moment before, rapidly cooled. Lonn felt the lack of it like a physical change, and he shivered. Nife stiffened, glanced between them, sensing the difference in mood.

Lonn ignored Llias' deliberate use of his first name. He was being provocative, and Lonn unclenched his jaw and tried very hard not to be provoked. "Llias, it is not safe for you here. The witch revealed herself to me: She is Lady Illt of Otharn, a most powerful and dangerous sorcerer."

"Did she say what she wanted, then?" Llias asked, as though it were an idle question.

"Yes, but I cannot speak it. It is—" He would not say it was an impossible task; he did not want Llias to react in fear. "—it is a weighty task that will not be fulfilled easily. If I fail, she will come for you."

"I can take care of myself," Llias said, indicating the bow and the *tanda*, "Thanks to your generosity."

"A bow is no defense against her!" Lonn said, frustrated that Llias refused his warnings and his protection.

"I am very good with it," Llias said evenly, "and with the *tanda*, as you have seen. I will not be tricked again, if that is what you are worried about. I will not come to Otharn, the very center of your empire! It is bad enough here with your guards on my heels at every moment." He pointed to the edge of the ring and sure enough, Ake and Varla were there.

"I ordered them to escort you for your own safety," Lonn said. He did not want to argue about this; Llias did not understand the danger he was in. "Otharn is far better defended than the garrison, my quarters are warded against all threats, arcane and otherwise—"

Llias cut him off, his color rising, "*Your* quarters? Lonn, what exactly are you proposing? I told you I will not sit on your—"

"Enough!" Lonn snapped, his patience at an end. Nife looked as though he wished the ground would open at his feet, and even Hilde was having trouble keeping her expression under control. Lonn took a deep breath. "Enough," he repeated in his most reasonable tone. "Do not argue with me Llias, I have made my decision."

Llias gaped at him in shock. "Do not argue with you?" he said, incredulous. "You are no better than that witch! She took me against my will and now you do the same thing."

"I will send the tribute to Fryst, as we agreed—" Lonn began, but again Llias cut him off.

"We did *not* agree!" Llias said, a purple blush rising on his cheeks, his deep eyes flashing in anger. "You did not give me the chance to agree, and it seems that my agreement is irrelevant. You wish to keep me as your prisoner? Or do you think me your slave? You paid a high price for me, after all!"

Lonn's temper was boiling over, and it was lucky that they were interrupted at that moment by a shout from the far side of the training grounds. It was one of Lonn's outriders, a member of the mounted patrols that circled the garrison in wide loops, alert for any signs of trouble. Someone was on the horse behind her, and they were approaching fast. Off-duty soldiers jumped out of their path.

"My prince," the rider said as she reined her horse before the group. "I bring you an arrival from Otharn. She said it was urgent, and she has your token."

Nife hurried forward to help the second rider down from the horse. Whoever it was, she was clearly unused to being on horseback, as she nearly fell into Nife's firm hold. The guard stepped aside and Lonn saw who had arrived in such a rush. A page girl, breathless and disheveled, her hair bundled up in a black scarf. She looked familiar, but the dark-red uniform was not one that Lonn knew.

"What is it, girl?" Hilde snapped, getting right to the point as always.

By way of answer, the girl reached into her jacket. Hilde and Nife both put their hands on their swords, Ake and Varla ghosting up behind them. They all watched the girl as she slowly and carefully pulled a scrap of cloth from her pocket. Lonn frowned. It was burned and stained, but unmistakably the sky-blue color of his signature cape. He had only given such tokens to two people: Darrin Gulna Oxi of Otharn, and David Thomen of Earth.

"Where did you get that?" Lonn demanded as Illt's words about his brother surged to the forefront of his mind. Only bad news was delivered with such a bloody token.

The girl curtsied and held out the scrap of cloth, her other hand behind her back. "Darrin Gulna Oxi sent me, my prince," she said, her voice so low that he had to strain to hear her. She was nervous, surrounded by armed guards and standing before the crown prince himself, but she spoke her message, "I bring word from him. It is about your brother, Prince Vell."

# Messenger

"Tell me everything," Lonn ordered when they had relocated to his command pavilion in the center of the garrison. There was a long, map-strewn table but no chairs; Lonn did not like to encourage lingering in discussions and arguments.

The girl swallowed nervously, looking at the faces surrounding her: Lonn himself, of course, Captains Hilde and Rillen, and Lieutenant Ake. Llias was there as well, unwillingly, as Lonn refused to let him out of his sight. He sighed at the lack of comforts and folded his arms, leaning against a tent-pole.

"I am Erla," the girl started, and as she spoke her name, Lonn realized that he knew her. He had met her many times before in his brother's chambers, delivering his messages, bringing his refreshments, or sitting at his table, transcribing notes.

"You were my brother's page," he said, the spark of alarm at her sudden appearance turning to something else. Not hope, exactly, but a feeling that connections were being made, that the long thread that bound events together was finally coming into his view.

She nodded. "Yes, my prince. I was Prince Vell's page for three years, before he left Otharn for the first time." She paused and clenched her fist at her side. The first time Vell had left Otharn had been to conceal his spirit-daughter's whereabouts from the king. The second time he had left had been in chains on his way to Vaaladir as a slave. Erla steadied herself and continued, "I stayed at the palace after that as a maid. I had nowhere else to go, and I never thought to see him again. But ten days ago, he returned."

"Returned?" Lonn questioned, his eyebrows raised.

"Not of his own choice, my prince," Erla said. "He was brought back by Lady Illt and her mages, and Lord David Thomen of Earth was brought too."

Erla told her tale, growing more confident as she got through it. She only faltered when she said that Vell had been cursed with the *nehu* rune — a slave tattoo that gave the one who controlled it great power over the unfortunate victim. When she said that, the edge of the table cracked under Lonn's fist. As far as he knew, the *nehu* rune was irreversible, and he had little doubt which powerful sorcerer had forced it on his brother. A long silence fell as everyone held their breath, waiting for the Prince's temper to either flare up or subside, but Llias spoke into the silence.

"You're scaring her," he said, his voice low and calm, his easy pose unchanged, leaning on the post, his arms loosely folded.

"I am *not*," Lonn said through clenched teeth. He let go of the table. It was only a flimsy thing anyway. Breaking it was not enough to scare anyone.

"Control yourself," Llias said, unimpressed by Lonn's glare. Hilde shifted on her feet, ready to escort this irreverent Fryst out of the prince's sight, but Lonn held up his hand. He paused for a moment, let the warmth of Llias' presence work its magic. The connection was still there, and Lonn was inexplicably calmed and comforted by it. Llias was his familiar, Illt had said, but Lonn did not know what that meant. That was a question for another time, though.

Now, he took a deep breath and nodded to Erla, who was watching him with dark, wide eyes, "Carry on."

She did, finishing her tale with Vell and David's fiery escape through the *fjarleoth*, which lined up with what Illt had told him. Lonn was surprised that Illt had not embellished her version, but he supposed it was dramatic enough without any additions.

"After that," Erla said, her hand nervously tucking her tight curls back under her scarf, "Darrin took me to work for the stable master. He told me to stay out of the palace. The king was angry...." She trailed off, and Lonn could only imagine the white-heat of his father's rage at Vell's escape. She swallowed and told the rest of it: "He had Darrin whipped. He took his axe and his rights as a warrior. He is barred from the training grounds and from the armory. Darrin said the king would have done worse had he not had this."

She pointed at the scrap of cloth in Lonn's fist.

"The king is using the *fjarleoth* to scry the land and no one can travel," she went on. "He must think that Vell is still on Otharn; soldiers are searching everywhere for him. Lady Illt was banished and the big *fjarleoth* at the plaza cracked and broke after she stepped through it. There are new guards everywhere, and people are afraid. Darrin came to me last night and gave me your token, and told me to deliver his message to you. He would not come because he is watched, and he fears the king is not done with him. The portal site is guarded but the guards don't care about ..." She paused to breathe, the whole tent hanging on her words. "They don't care about *some silly girl,* so I cried and told them that I was scared and homesick. I gave them what coin I had, and they let me pass."

Erla paused, gasping for breath at the end of her tale, her face flushed, the fingers of her hand trembling as she still tucked and re-tucked her hair.

"What is Darrin's message?" Lonn asked, although he could already guess the answer from what Erla had said.

She looked down at her feet. "Darrin is afraid that the king...that the king is not in his right mind," she said, her voice small as she dared to voice such disrespect before the crown prince. "He begs you to come home."

Silence fell. Lonn just waited, absorbing the information and letting it settle into his mind. His captains, used to his ways, waited too. The prince would let them know when he wanted to hear their thoughts, but their well-practiced routine was interrupted by Llias.

"The witch Illt is here, on Tornatt," he informed Erla. "She took me from Fryst three days ago, and she has her hooks in Lonn for some favor he can't speak of."

"He cannot speak of it?" Erla asked, her brow furrowed.

Llias waved his hand, ignoring Lonn's dark glare. "He swore an oath so the witch wouldn't kill me, but it's probably safe to assume the favor is related to her banishment from Otharn and the associated events."

"Pardon me, sir, but who are you?" Erla asked, unsure why she and this man were having this conversation in front of the prince and his captains.

Llias gave her a smile and a short bow. "I am Llias, *ishaxha* of Fryst. I am Lonn's prisoner."

Lonn growled at that and Llias offered him a pleasant smile. "Am I not?" he asked, one eyebrow raised.

Hilde threw Lonn a meaningful look, one that conveyed without words that the stockade was still very much an option. Lonn would be lying if he said he was not tempted, except that the thought of being that far away from Llias was intolerable.

That aside, his decision seemed obvious enough: Vell, his children, the king, Lady Illt, Llias — Lonn could not see the connections yet, but they were there, and they all converged on his home world.

"I will return to Otharn at once," he said. "Rillen, you have command of the garrison."

Before Rillen could acknowledge the order, Llias clapped his hands together, seemingly oblivious to the glares he was collecting. "It sounds like you have everything worked out, so I will be on my way."

Before anyone could stop him, Llias turned and strode from the tent. Lonn didn't wait for Hilde to bring him back. He was out of time and out of patience with these games. He followed Llias and grabbed him by the shoulder, holding him by a fistful of his shirt. "You will come with me," he said. "Hilde, join me on Otharn as soon as you can."

Before Hilde could open her mouth to agree, or Llias to protest, Lonn summoned Skarpur, opened a portal back to Otharn, and he and Llias fell through it.

# Otharn

Llias yelled in alarm as the portal opened under his feet and he fell. There was nothing to hold on to but Lonn himself, and the chill barrier between them dropped as fast as they did. Llias grabbed Lonn's shoulders and Lonn wrapped a strong arm around his waist, holding him close. The threads of Lonn's arcane power protected Llias, shielding him from the intensity of the journey through the crystal realm. Without Llias' resistance, their connection was painfully strong when they arrived on Otharn. They landed hard on the plaza and both lost their balance, the power surging between them like a choppy sea. Lonn's injured knee twisted under him and he was forced to lean on Llias rather than the other way around.

With a muttered curse, Llias caught his balance and shoved Lonn off him, sending the prince staggering back, falling over his own feet and ending up on his backside on the flagstones. Lonn sprawled on the ground, smiling despite his undignified landing. The twin suns above them lit Llias' face in overlapping orange and purple light, glowing on his blue skin and lighting up his deep blue eyes as if they were jewels.

"Welcome to Otharn," Lonn said with an expansive gesture, taking in the travel plaza, the palace and city spread out below them, and the fields and forest beyond.

For a moment the exhilaration of their journey lasted, the bond flowing between them. It was over too fast, though. As soon as Llias steadied himself, Lonn's magic was shoved aside, flowing around and past Llias like an immovable boulder in a river, unable to gain any purchase on him. Llias stepped back and folded his arms.

"My new prison?" he asked, looking around with a sniff. "I prefer the old one."

Lonn glanced around too. The arrival square was usually bustling at this time of day, but now it was silent. He looked over his shoulder, towards the center of the plaza. Just as Erla had said, the huge travel stone that had stood there for generations was cracked clean in half. Lonn had never seen such a thing; the interior of the stone was a web of broken crystal shards, some of it crumbled to dust. It had been left where it had fallen, with no attempt to repair it or even to clear the damage. Lonn got to his feet. Three plaza guards were heading towards them, swords drawn.

"Peace," Lonn said at their suspicious faces. "Do you not know me?"

"Identify yourself!" the lead guard barked, a weasel-faced man with a punched-in nose. Lonn frowned, his good temper at seeing his home evaporating like so much water.

"Lower your weapons and have a care how you speak to your prince!" he said, hardly able to believe that his father's guard greeted him in such a manner.

"Who is this?" weasel-face demanded, pointing at Llias, but Lonn was in no mood to be interrogated. He opened his mouth to give the man a piece of his mind, but Llias was already speaking.

"Greetings," he said with a short bow. "I am Llias, ishaxha of Fryst and Lonn's prisoner."

Lonn thought he would break his teeth from clenching his jaw. He turned to Llias, slow and deliberate. "Stop introducing yourself like that," he gritted out, pausing between each word.

There must have been a wild look in his eyes, because Llias did not make his usual argument that he was only speaking the truth. He wisely kept his mouth shut, and Lonn turned back to weasel-face, who was too stupid to pay attention to the exchange.

"Why is your prisoner armed?" the guard asked, his eyes narrowed. "Prove you are truly Prince Lonn. Where are your guards? Where are your colors?"

Lonn raised Skarpur, which somehow the irritating man had failed to notice. He noticed it now, though, and took a step back, the blood rushing from his face. Lonn let the blade hover before his nose.

"How dare you speak to me in such a way?" Lonn hissed, his temper rising. "I should give that ugly nose of yours a brand-new shape. It couldn't be any worse than the one you already have."

"My prince!" the man stammered, his two friends leaning away from him, leaving him without support in the face of Lonn's wrath. "My apologies. The king has ordered none may use the *fjarleoth* to travel from other worlds, I did not...I did not..."

"No, you did *not*," Lonn growled, taking a deliberate step towards the cowering man. Finally, here was a righteous target for his pent-up anger that was neither a powerful sorcerer nor his fated arcane partner. Finally, he did not need to hold back. Power sparked on Skarpur's blade, and the man yelped and fell, scrambling backwards as Lonn advanced on him.

"Lonn," Llias said, his voice low.

Lonn paused as though he had reached an invisible barrier. He shook his head, anger dissipating. The pathetic guard was not worth his time, and Lonn left him to his whimpering. He had more important business to attend to. He had to understand the reason for this deserted plaza, for the broken travel stone, for the aggressive welcome. Things were not well on Otharn, as Erla had indicated. There was no time to dawdle out in the open. His most important task was to get Llias to safety.

"Come," he said, and before Llias could react Lonn hooked his arm around his waist again and raised his spear.

"No, no flying!" Llias protested, shoving at Lonn's chest to get him off, but Lonn just tightened his grip.

"Hold on," he said, and their feet left the ground.

Llias did hold on, although he had little choice about it. Lonn was sure he dug his nails in harder than he had to as they soared over the city of sparkling grey stone. Lonn looked down at his beloved city; it was only afternoon but the street and squares were as quiet as the travel plaza had been. Only a few people hurried about their business, alone. The cafes and open-air taverns were almost deserted.

They landed on Lonn's balcony high in a tower above the palace. As soon as he could, Llias shoved Lonn away again, both physically and with his arcane power. He stumbled back, one hand pressed to his side where Lonn's hand had been, leaning against the wall, his face pale. Lonn froze. His injury — the ugly cut where the witch had wounded him. The flight must have re-opened it.

"Llias, sit down," Lonn said, guilt boiling up inside him. He pulled a chair close, holding out his hand for Llias to steady himself.

Llias stepped back. "Don't touch me."

He ignored the chair and the proffered hand. Taking a deep breath, he looked around Lonn's rooms, ignoring the magnificent view over the city and beyond.

"Why have you brought me here, Lonn?" he demanded. "These are your rooms, are they not? Your private chambers? What are you—?" He paused and shuddered, his hand pressed to his side, the white of his borrowed shirt stained with dark blood.

Lonn jumped forward. "You are hurt, please sit. I will find a healer."

"I do not need a healer," Llias snapped. "I need you to leave me alone!"

Llias backed away from Lonn until he found a door behind him. Without taking his eyes off the prince, he opened it, stepped through and slammed it behind him. Lonn sighed. It was his bedroom door that Llias had fled through, and of course he was welcome to use it, to rest and use the attached bathing rooms, but Lonn could certainly not follow him in there. Not if he didn't want Llias to think the very worst of him.

Lonn leaned on the railing of the balcony and looked glumly out at his world.

He was home.

# Goodnight

The golden-orange glory of Sinugult's sunset was already over when there was a soft tap at the inner door to Lonn's chambers.

"Come," he said, and the door opened to reveal the page Erla.

Tense and anxious, she curtsied. "Pardon me, my prince. I am sorry to disturb you. I returned with your guards and..."

"What is it?" Lonn said, more harshly than he had intended. Over the girl's shoulder he could see Nife and Myrun at their posts outside the outer door. Between the inner and outer doors, there was a reception room, scattered with chairs and small tables. It was a waiting area, where visitors to the prince's chambers could cool their heels and await his pleasure. Lonn rarely made use of it.

Erla chewed her lip and looked at the ground, and Lonn realized why she had come. She had nowhere else to go.

"Where is Darrin?" he asked in a softer tone.

"He is not in his rooms, my prince," Erla said, "Perhaps he is out in the city, or with a friend — but I do not know. I do not think he would leave the palace, after he sent me to find you."

"Come in, then," Lonn said, closing the inner door behind her. Lonn had no page of his own.

He had never cared to have one either, sending his guards on whatever errands he could not run himself. He didn't like to have people fussing about him, and from what he could tell pages excelled at fussing. But this girl had been Vell's, and Darrin had trusted her with his token and his treasonous message. Lonn owed her for that. He owed her his protection and a place to sleep, at least.

"You can stay with me for now. Find Darrin in the morning and bring him here. Llias will need a page, anyway, at least at first."

Erla looked around the room, at the gleaming crystal-embedded stone walls and plain wood furnishings. There was no unnecessary embellishment anywhere. It was plain and simple, a soldier's room.

"Where is L...your guest, my prince?" she asked.

"You can call him Llias." Lonn sighed, running a hand through thick, dark-blond hair, his stress and tiredness making him candid. "He calls me Lonn. Apparently, we're all on a first-name basis now."

"Yes, my prince," Erla said, shuffling her feet, unsure what to make of Lonn's gloomy confession. "But where is he?"

Lonn pointed at his bedroom door, from whence not a sound had come since Llias had slammed it hours before.

Erla paused, choosing her words carefully. "Will Llias require a guest room, my prince? Or will he be staying here? With you?"

A guest room would be appropriate, but Lonn only considered it for a moment before he shook his head. He could not allow Llias to be too far away. The lure of their bond was too great, and Lonn needed him to be close. "He will stay here," he decided.

"In your bedroom, my prince?" Erla looked away, but she dared to challenge him, however mildly.

The girl was right, and Lonn found he had warmed to her already. He was not thinking straight; he could not propose that option. Llias had been very clear about his lack of interest, and he would be wary about Lonn keeping him too close. Luckily, Erla had a suggestion.

"How about your study?" she asked, pointing to the open door on the other side of the living area. "It seems a good size. I can ask the housekeepers to..."

"Do it."

Lonn didn't even let her finish, already pleased with his decision to let her stay. He would have to keep her out of his father's way, but that should not be too hard. It seemed that the king had far more to worry about than the whereabouts of a single page girl. Such as, perhaps, the whereabouts of Darrin Gulna Oxi. Lonn had a high level of confidence in Darrin's ability to navigate through difficult situations at the court. He had survived for many years on his own wits and charm, but he had never before gone directly against the king. Lonn would be more worried if Darrin did not have the habit of spending his nights with a variety of pleasant company. If he was not to be found in the morning, Lonn would worry about him then.

Erla curtsied and hurried off. Before the purple disk of Foubla had touched the horizon, she was back, leading a parade of housekeepers and porters. Lonn retreated to the balcony while they moved his heavy desk out into a corner of the living area and converted the study into a cozy bedroom. Erla neatly stacked up all his ignored papers and documents and put them on the center of the desk under a heavy paperweight. The paperweight was a metal statue of a fierce *halfor* that Vell had made for him long ago, melting and casting the metal himself. It was one of Lonn's most precious items, along with the fur of the same beast they had hunted together in the royal forest of Otharn. Lonn wondered if Erla recognized it and had chosen it for that reason.

Erla left a tray of food on the sideboard and shooed the last of the housekeepers out, shutting the inner door behind her with a one-handed curtsy. She could sleep on a couch in the reception room until Lonn found a better arrangement for her.

Lonn peeked into the new bedroom. He had to admit, the girl had done a good job. The palace was full of furniture. It would have been no problem to find a bed and dresser, a comfortable chair and bookcase for Llias, but Erla had also added extra touches to make the room cozy. There was a rug on the floor and a selection of books on the shelf. The bedspread was Lonn's sky-blue color, which made him smile. Llias would be sleeping under his colors, and there was something very satisfying about that. It pleased the possessive part of Lonn's nature that already considered Llias to be his.

Everything was ready, and Lonn had no further reason to wait. He tapped on Llias' door. *His* door, he corrected himself. It was the door to his own bedroom and he was a prince waiting outside like a supplicant! He tried to wrangle his irritation as he waited, but his fist had risen to knock again when Llias snatched the door open.

"Yes?" he said, his eyebrows raised as though Lonn were a mildly inconvenient visitor. He had taken off his quiver and his borrowed boots, and he seemed to have made himself at home.

When Lonn was sure his voice would not come out as an outraged growl he said, "Llias, are you feeling better?" He indicated the dark bloodstain on Llias' shirt, thankfully small. Stuffed under the shirt, the bulk of a makeshift bandage made with one of Lonn's towels reassured him that Llias was well.

"It's fine," Llias said, covering the area with his hand.

"It is late," Lonn said after a moment of silence which Llias clearly had no intention of filling, "Would you care to see your room?"

Llias folded his arms and leaned on the doorframe. "*This* isn't my room, then?" He gestured behind him at Lonn's uncluttered bedroom; the bed hung with sky blue drapes, the white *halfor* pelt on the floor as a rug, everything clean and sleek and polished against the sparkling crystal-inset walls.

"No, Llias," Lonn replied, certain that Llias was deliberately antagonizing him. "This is *my* room."

The now-familiar threads of Lonn's magic wound themselves around Llias as he stood there, almost without Lonn noticing it. Llias didn't give any indication that he was aware of it. Lonn was glad that whenever Llias relaxed; the bond grew. It only became cold and shrank when Llias was deliberately pushing it away. Left to its own devices, the bond drew them together.

"The bed is very comfortable," Llias said with a yawn. His fake yawn turned into a real one and he stretched his arms over his head.

The opening was too much for Lonn to resist. "If you find the bed comfortable Llias," he said, leaning closer and lowering his voice, "you are welcome to share it with me. You will find me most accommodating."

Llias grinned and quickly covered it up with a frown. He was not fast enough to fool Lonn, who was delighted at his reaction. Perhaps

Llias had just needed to rest from his journey through the portal. It was a difficult experience for those unused to it, and Llias still must also be affected by his ordeal with the witch. That would explain his bad mood at their arrival.

"I think not," Llias said in an imperious tone, ducking back into Lonn's room to pick up his boots and his weapons. "Very well, if this is your room, show me to *my* room."

Lonn was surprised Llias didn't snap his fingers as he issued his order, and he hid his smile with an elegant bow as he waved his *guest* through the door.

"This way," he said, directing him across the living room to his former study. He felt a flutter of hope in his chest that Llias might be warming to him. It seemed he could not keep in a bad temper with Lonn, despite the prince whisking him away from Tornatt and refusing to let him return to Fryst.

Lonn opened the door for him but did not cross the threshold. He would not, unless he were invited. He might be somewhat rough around the edges, but he was not so ill-mannered as *that*. His magic was warm and bubbling under his skin as Llias entered the room, looking around, eventually setting down his weapons and nodding his approval.

"I suppose as jail cells go, this is not so bad," Llias allowed.

"I am glad you like it," Lonn said, with another smile. "If there is anything you desire to make your jail more comfortable, Erla will be happy to assist you."

Llias bit his lip and seemed to consider his words before he said them. "I have had worse cells than this, and I have had *far* worse jailers than you, Lonn, but that is what this is, and it is what *you* are. I will not forget it, however charming you may be."

Slowly, and more painful because it was slow, Llias pushed Lonn's arcane energy away. He shoved it from him like a plow until there was nothing left but an empty, echoing chasm between them.

"Goodnight, Lonn," Llias said, and shut the door in his face.

# Welcome

Early the next morning, Erla went to fetch breakfast and returned with Lonn's dear friend Darrin Gulna Oxi on her heels. Darrin held out his arms, and Lonn rolled his eyes but let himself be embraced. Darrin was one of very few who could take such liberties, and he usually seemed to enjoy Lonn's irritation with him. This time, however, his smile was tight and his posture stiff, his usually bright white jacket was dusty and blotched, and his grey trousers the same. He looked as though he had slept in his clothes, and Lonn held him at arm's length, inspecting him as he gripped his shoulders tightly.

"You are well, Darrin?" Lonn asked.

Darrin shrugged, "Well enough," he said, avoiding Lonn's piercing gaze. "I am lying low at present. The king is displeased with me, as you might guess, and I am trying to stay beneath his notice."

"And?" Lonn asked, knowing that was far from the full story, "What else?" He brushed at Darrin's jacket, rubbing his fingers over the stains on it. Darrin stepped back, self-conscious at his unusually shabby appearance.

"I am staying away from my rooms," he admitted. "Your dear brother left me with numerous bills, and then your father took away my income. So I must tell you, my friend, times are hard. While your guards were gone, I have been staying in their barracks."

Lonn frowned, "Why did you not pay the bills from my accounts?" he asked, pulling the burned and stained sky-blue strip of cloth from his pocket and giving it back to his friend. "Is my token no longer good in this place?"

Darrin took the crumbling cloth and smoothed it between his fingers. "Well," he said, a slight smirk crossing his face. "Jjon Ul has more reason than ever to dislike me now. He would not accept your token in such poor condition. He refused to allow me to draw on your accounts, and although he was in the wrong, I thought it unwise to take my case to the king."

"What reason—" Lonn started, wondering how Darrin had managed to antagonize the prickly palace seneschal even more than he usually did, but then he decided that it was irrelevant. Darrin had been carrying out Lonn's business and using his accounts for years. It certainly was not Jjon Ul's place to stop him, but without Lonn there to enforce his wishes, and without the king to turn to, Darrin had little recourse.

"I see," Lonn said instead, his blood pressure rising. "Fine. Jjon Ul doesn't like my token? My father has my friend sleeping in the guard room and my brother's allies hiding in the stables?" He gestured toward Erla, and the girl looked wide-eyed at being called an ally of the prince. "Very well then. Let us be very clear about the meaning of these actions," Lonn concluded.

The prince stomped to his room, his anger building, the confinement of the palace already pressing down on him. He had hardly turned his back, and in his absence the shaky peace he had built up with his parents seemed to have been utterly disregarded and torn down. It was as though they had been waiting for him to leave to try to trap his brother once again — and if not for Darrin and Erla, they would have succeeded. Lonn rummaged in his cabinets and pulled out a few items.

"Put this on," he said, tossing Darrin his own cape of sky-blue cloth. "And you can have this," he told Erla, holding up a silk shirt, also in sky-blue. "Take off that black." With a quick wrench, he tore off the sleeves and collar of the shirt, making a roughly rectangular scarf. The edges were uneven and already fraying, but Erla took it as though it was woven from gold.

"Yes, my prince," she said, and vanished into the reception room. She reappeared a moment later with her scruffy black scarf gone and her hair smoothly tied up in blue silk.

Lonn looked from one to the other, both wearing his colors, their allegiance made perfectly clear. He folded his arms. He was tired of these lies and deceptions, and he would not tolerate them any longer. Anyone now who harassed Darrin or Erla would do so under no doubt they were defying Lonn himself.

Darrin was the first to speak. He strolled over to the breakfast tray, his new cape slung over one shoulder. "So, where is your guest?" he asked, taking a piece of fruit and a cup of *kurvorur*.

Lonn sighed. "You know about him, then?"

He should not be surprised, Darrin knew everything that happened in the palace. His new constrained circumstances did not appear to have changed that at all.

"The entire palace and much of the city knows about him, my friend. Rumors are running wild, tales of you flying over the city with a handsome and exotic man in your arms. Some off-world paramour, perhaps?"

Lonn wrinkled his nose, amused despite himself. "You thought me with my paramour, but still came here before Foubla has even risen?" That was an exaggeration, both suns had risen, but Foubla, the purple sun of the evening, had been up less than an hour.

Darrin gave his friend a look. "You should thank me, hmm? I *could* have come last night!" His expression turned serious. "Who is he, Lonn? I have known you for many years, and I have never known you to bring a lover to your own bed in the palace. Or be seen in public with one, or, indeed, to spend time with one who does not want to be paid."

"All right!" Lonn retorted. His habits were a favorite topic of Darrin's teasing, but his heart was not in it that morning. "He is here, sleeping," He pointed at the door of the study, and Darrin gave him a confused look. "He is not in my bedroom because he is not my paramour!" Lonn explained. "He is...something else."

*"I'm his prisoner."*

The voice came from the balcony, and they all spun to see Llias in the doorway, a book tucked under his arm. He was wearing the same clothes he had worn the day before, tiredness still clear on his face, the bloodstain still showing on his white shirt. Lonn realized Llias had nothing else to wear. He would have to do something about that, and quickly. He had more shirts in sky-blue, but Llias deserved to have his own clothes, tailored to fit.

"Llias!" Lonn exclaimed. "How long have you been out there?" Lonn thought himself an early riser but Llias must have been up before him.

Llias gave him a dark look. "Oh, I'm sorry. Am I to stay in my cell until you release me? You know, I am sure you could get a bolt for the door and lock me in at night, if that's your preference."

Lonn ground his teeth. "Darrin, this is Llias. He is *not* a prisoner. There is much to tell, but he and I have an arcane bond. It is not safe for him to leave."

Llias held his gaze for a long moment and turned to Darrin, "Hello. I'm Llias, *ishaxha* of Fryst. Lonn bought me from a witch at the Varhin market and he won't let me go." He held out his hand.

Darrin clasped it, his eyebrows so high on his head they had practically vanished.

"Darrin Gulna Oxi," he said automatically. "Well met."

"Gulna Oxi," Llias said, thoughtfully, looking Darrin over. "*Golden Axe.* I wouldn't expect a man to have a name like that without the weapon in question."

"Ahh," Darrin said, the tension back in his posture, the tightness around his eyes different from his usual relaxed demeanor. "You are right. I earned that name in battle, but it seems since recent events I no longer have the right to it."

"You're the one who sent Erla to Tornatt," Llias realized.

"Indeed, I am," Darrin said. "Lonn, it seems we have more to discuss than I thought, hmm?"

With a heartfelt groan, Lonn rubbed his hands through his hair. "We do. But I must visit my mother this morning and get her side of this tangled story. I cannot believe it is any coincidence that Vell was brought here almost as soon as I left."

"Aye," Darrin said. "The queen will be in her gardens. The rumor is that she has not left them since Vell escaped, that she is consumed by her visions. I will walk with you." He turned to Llias, whose curious eyes still lingered on him. "Llias, a pleasure to meet you," he said with a short bow.

Llias nodded. "Likewise. Come back anytime and fill me in about *recent events* if you like, Darrin. I will do the same."

Before Darrin could agree, Lonn grabbed his shoulder and steered him towards the door. Llias gave them a lazy wave and headed back out to the balcony, opening his book. Lonn considered for a moment and turned back. "Llias, Erla has brought breakfast, and she will bring you anything else that you want or need. Do not leave these rooms."

Llias just smiled, and Lonn paused. "I will have your word you will not leave these rooms," he said cautiously.

Llias laughed at that. "You will *not* have my word, Lonn. If you wish to keep prisoners, you'd better guard them."

Lonn clenched his jaw and ignored Darrin's poorly hidden amusement. He strode to the outer door and found Ake and Myrun there.

"My guest will not leave my rooms," he ordered and left, the chill of Llias' disapproval chasing him down the hallway.

# Anlira

Darrin caught up to Lonn a few paces down the hallway.

"You have your hands full there," he murmured, but Lonn did not reply.

Once out of the protective wards of Lonn's chambers, they did not speak of anything of consequence. It was an old habit. There were always listeners in the palace, and Lonn's rooms were shielded by ancient wards, built into the very stones of the royal suite itself.

Instead, Lonn told Darrin of his time on Tornatt, the battles with the raiders that he had fought and won. Lonn was always fond of retelling his own victories, and Darrin was a good audience. The raiders had presented little challenge, and as Lonn retold it, his suspicion grew about why he had gone there in the first place. The messages from Tornatt had painted a far more dire threat than Lonn had found when he arrived.

They parted at the entrance to the queen's garden. Darrin declined to accompany him further and Lonn did not blame him. If Queen Anlira was half as wrath with Darrin as King Covl was, Darrin was wise to stay out of their way for a time.

"I will speak with you later," Lonn promised. He clasped Darrin's wrist as they parted, the sky-blue cape fluttering over Darrin's shoulder as he walked away.

Lonn walked through the queen's garden. He was such a frequent visitor to the place that his feet found his own way. The deep grove was as it ever was: bells and tinkling chimes hanging from the trees, large gray cats slinking through the shadows, glimpses of hidden clearings, buildings and statues off the cleared paths, distant views that seemed to change every time Lonn walked by.

He reached the center of the garden and found Queen Anlira alone by her golden harp. The mist from the waterfall decorated the strings like diamonds, and Anlira's fingers moved over them in a slow, hypnotic rhythm. Her eyes were distant, and Lonn lingered at the edge of the clearing, unsure if he had been seen or not.

"Mother," he said, and the queen looked up, the strings twanging tunelessly under her fingers, her focus broken.

"Lonn!" she said, a mix of relief and anxiety in her voice.

Lonn entered the clearing. The atmosphere that had seemed calming and peaceful when he was younger now felt cloying, and buzzed against his senses. The babble of waterfall, the noise of the chimes, the intent gaze of the yellow-eyed cats all pushed at his nerves, distracting and irritating him.

"Mother," he repeated, standing before her harp, arms folded. Now that he was here, he hardly even knew what to say, or what he could force himself to address without losing his temper and shouting at her.

"You wish to berate me about Vell," Anlira said, resting her fingers back on the strings of her harp, poised but not yet playing.

Lonn clenched his jaw. "Yes. I do wish to berate you, and I would if I thought it would do the slightest bit of good! What were you thinking? Vell was on Earth doing no harm to anyone, and he should have remained there."

Anlira plucked a single string of her harp, sending a clear, crystal note vibrating through the clearing, tiny droplets of water falling from the instrument like rain. "He conceived another monster," she said, her eyes losing focus again. "Your father saw it and he had to act at once."

Lonn shook his head, the note hanging in the air longer than it should have, filling his ears and driving out his thoughts.

"You should have waited for me," he said finally. "Children are not born overnight. There was time, I could have..." He paused. What would he had done, if he had been there when the king had discovered Vell's condition? He did not know, and he was selfishly relieved that he had not had to make that choice. "I could have talked to him."

Anlira touched another string, creating a second, complementary note to join the first. "My vision did not show me that path."

Lonn grabbed her hand as it moved to a third string, stopping her from playing it. "There is more to consider than just visions, mother. Vell is your son and my brother! David Thomen is my ally and friend, and you have made him an enemy of Otharn. Did your vision show you the consequences of that?"

"He is human," Anlira protested. "He is weak, short-lived, limited."

"Aye, he is all that and more," Lonn snapped. "And yet he and Vell defeated Lady Illt in this very city, and now they have vanished from your sight. Did you see that in your visions?"

The queen did not answer; instead, she looked down to Lonn's hand, gripping hers. "You seem different. What has happened to you on Tornatt? Who is that man you brought back with you?"

Lonn huffed and let go of her hand. He had not gone there to talk about Llias, about finding his familiar, about the new depths of power he could feel on the edge of his senses. He did not even want to tell her about his meeting with Illt and his promise to her. He did not trust her with any of that knowledge; it would be nothing but a distraction from what he needed to discuss.

"It is no matter," he said curtly. "What has father been doing since Vell and David left? The travel plaza is deserted and guarded by men I have never seen before. Is it true that no one may use the *fjarleoth*?"

Anlira nodded, her face serene. "Your father takes my visions seriously. He seeks your brother through the *fjarleoth*, and his only desire is to avert the tragedy that awaits us all if those children are allowed to live. Children are not born overnight, but the monster Vell calls Jormuna came into this world at only a quarter of her term. This one may too. Your father could not risk waiting."

"Jormuna was only born that way because of father's rash actions!" Lonn said, frustrated at his mother's refusal to see her own part in provoking these events. "And if you have done nothing at all these past days Vell would still be on Earth and his babe would still be in his belly." Everything she and the king had done to Vell had driven him and his children further away from their influence, and still she would not stop. She would not see reason; she only saw her visions.

Anlira gently drew her fingers across the strings of her harp, the notes again hanging in the air around Lonn's ears.

"Speak with your father if you must," she said. "The future is far from certain. Change surrounds us, and fate is watching. Choose your path wisely, my son."

The discussion was over, and Lonn left the clearing before his mother's music muddled his mind any further. He must be unusually sensitive to it today; usually he found it calming. As he left, the queen watched him. She strummed the strings with the hand that Lonn had held, listening carefully to the resulting chord. A slight frown crossed her face and she stroked the strings again and again. She tilted her head and closed her eyes, as though reaching for a note that was just out of her hearing.

# Escape

Lonn headed back to his quarters, deep in thought. His mother had not told him anything he did not already know. All she had done was layer her justifications on top of each other. Her visions often were predictive, true, but Lonn could not get rid of the feeling that there was more to this one than the queen understood.

It predicted the end of the joined realms — surely there was more to it than just the birth of Vell's children? He had no answers, and when he arrived the outer door, he checked in with Nife and Ake before he entered.

"Your...*guest*...was hungry, my prince. Erla has gone to fetch him some food."

Lonn nodded at Ake's report. Just as his captain and Nife had done, his lieutenant had no idea how to refer to Llias. As far as they knew, he was a slave, purchased half-dead from the Varhin market. As such, he was far beneath the notice of the prince's personal guard. But at the same time, the prince clearly valued him, keeping him in his personal chambers, tolerating his disrespect, allowing him to use the services of a page when it should be the other way around. Lonn would have to clarify things at some point, but it was not something he could even explain to himself. Not yet.

He entered his chambers and stopped by the inner door. The stillness in the air felt wrong, and Lonn's awareness of Llias' presence was not as intense as it should be. Llias' bedroom door was open, and Lonn knew at once that Llias was not there. The arcane compass of his heart pulled Lonn out to the balcony, and he looked over the edge; a long, twisted rope of silk sheets led to the balcony underneath his. Lonn cursed and summoned Skarpur, dropping down and landing lightly on the tile. The level below his in the tower was empty, kept for use by occasional honored guests. The door from the balcony into the guest suite had been forced open. Lonn ground his teeth and followed.

The guest suite was clean and almost bare. There were few furnishings and decorations, to better show off the wealth of crystal embedded in the stones. The door to the passageway outside was still closed, one of Llias' arrows jammed between the frame and the lock, the shaft broken off. Llias leaned against it, arms folded, frustration on his face.

"Lonn." He scowled, as though Lonn were the one intruding on him, as though he were not a slave caught in the act of running away — a crime that was punished as severely on Otharn as on any other world.

"Llias." Lonn sighed, relieved to see him despite his willfulness. The tendrils of his magic crept across the distance between them, wrapping around the runaway's ankles, seeking his presence like the flame seeks the fuel. "I believe you were going to stay in my rooms."

Llias shook his head. "No. You said you would have my word I wouldn't leave, and I very clearly remember refusing to give it."

"Well, you have had your fun, then," Lonn said, taking Llias by the arm. "Now we will return to my rooms, and you will stay there. Behave yourself and you will find me most reasonable. Do not, and you will not like the consequences."

Llias opened his mouth to argue but then shut it again, sensing the futility in speaking. At least this time, Lonn would have his way because he could enforce it.

"Fine," Llias said, deflating, "Take me back to jail. I couldn't unlock the door, anyway. Arrows are no good as lockpicks."

With a quick wrench, Lonn removed the broken arrow from the door, and opened the lock with a burst of energy from Skarpur. One hand on Llias' shoulder, he walked him back upstairs to his quarters. When they got there, Erla was just arriving with a laden tray. She and the guards stared as Lonn walked by with the man they were supposed to be guarding under his arm. Lonn handed Ake the broken arrow as he passed and took the tray from Erla.

"Double the guard," he said, closing the outer door behind them and letting Llias go ahead of him into the main room.

Llias had taken less than two hours to find his way out of Lonn's rooms, and the prince doubted this would be his last attempt. He took a lemon cake from Erla's tray and ate it in two bites. Taking a few moments to arrange his thoughts before facing Llias again would be wise. He took a deep breath and ate another cake. They were his favorites, and he wondered if the girl had known. Probably she did. The servants knew everything that happened in the palace, down to the smallest detail. With no other reason to delay, Lonn took a final, calming breath and walked through the inner door, setting the tray down on the table by Llias' chair.

Llias was not in the least intimidated. He lounged in Lonn's favorite chair and picked up a bread roll from the tray, breaking off pieces and eating them one by one. Lonn threw himself onto the couch opposite, glad at least that Llias was content enough to allow him to feel the warmth of his presence, to allow his magic to creep back to his side.

"Do I need to get you a collar and leash?" Lonn asked, his tone mild.

Llias choked on the mouthful he was eating. He sputtered for a moment and took a big gulp of water.

"Absolutely not!" he said, affronted. "Keep your fantasies to yourself."

Lonn leaned forward on his seat and took a handful of grapes from the tray. "Llias, do not try my patience. I have allowed you certain liberties, but I will only be pushed so far. You would not like me when I am angry."

Llias wrinkled his nose. "I don't like you *now*," he said, but there was no heat in it.

Lonn smiled at him. "You *do*," he said, certain that he was correct — that Llias did like him, despite his claim to the contrary. "You like me. And once you understand your position here, you will like me even better."

"I'll like you just fine if you let me go," Llias shot back, his gaze intent. "I'll even let you visit me on Fryst."

That would have been a tempting offer if it were not for Illt, but Llias would not be safe on Fryst if that witch were hunting him. He ate the grapes and waited for Llias to eat something too. When the man had at least eaten the bread he had pulled to pieces, Lonn started.

"Llias, there is something else I must tell you. Something important."

Llias chewed his last mouthful slowly. "Go on."

Lonn smiled. "You are my familiar." Lady Illt might be untrustworthy, but she had been right about that, Lonn could feel it in his heart.

Llias stared at him, blinking. "I'm your what?" he said, leaning forward, forgetting his quarrel with Lonn in his confusion.

"You are my familiar," Lonn repeated.

The words tasted sweet on his tongue; the truth of them rippled through his body and through the arcane energy that always surrounded him. Llias must have felt it too. Their energy was connected, and Llias had let down the barriers he had raised, allowing Lonn's power to surround him.

"No, I'm not," Llias said, but even his denial was half-questioning.

Drawn forward, Lonn reached out his hand and let it lie between them on the low table.

"You are," he said softly, "and I think you know it. I am a sorcerer; as little as I embrace it. And you are my arcane familiar, the heart and foundation of my power."

Llias did not take his offered hand. "Familiars are animals," he said shortly, his arms folded. "Not people. Even I know that."

"Nevertheless. It is what you are. It is the truth. It was fate that led me to you, and fate that will keep us together."

Lonn paused to let that information sink in. Llias was shaking his head, not accepting this truth, but Lonn had yet more to burden him with.

"Even more important," he continued, "for now no one must know. It is not safe yet."

Llias picked up another bread roll, chewed and swallowed it, thoughtful. "So, what are you going to tell people when they wonder why you're keeping me in your rooms? Apart from the obvious."

Lonn nodded. Llias was already ahead of him. "Yes, the obvious it is, I'm afraid. It is not the right time for my parents to know about you. They will want to meet you, to fit you into their plans. It is better for them to be ignorant for now. If they notice you at all, they will think you no more than my lover."

"Won't they wonder why you have to keep your lover locked up?"

"I am the crown prince of Otharn," Lonn shrugged. "It is not important if you are willing or not. If they question it at all, it will be to wonder why you do not accept this honor paid to you."

Llias stared at him, incredulous. He glanced at the open door of his room, where he had set down his bow and his *tanda*.

"No one will question you?" he said. "You know that, do you? You have done this before?"

"No!" Lonn said. "No, Llias, I have not." He made a decision to be as open and honest with Llias as possible, if he hoped to win his trust. "I do not do such things. I do not do *any* such things! In fact, it has been some time since..." Lonn let his words trail off with an awkward gesture. It was not as though he could freely choose his own company. Every person he met had an ulterior motive to be pleasant to him, to seduce him, to encourage his affection. On Tornatt, without the regular few courtesans who knew him and wanted to share his bed and take his money, he had been deprived of company for a while.

Llias scoffed. "That doesn't make me feel any better, Lonn. What if you get lonely? Don't think I haven't seen how you look at me, how you're always trying to sneak your magic on me."

Llias waved his hand and shoved Lonn's magic back and away from him, as casual as it was possible to be. Lonn shivered, the lack of connection cold where he had been warm and comfortable a moment before. Lonn had thought himself undetected as he allowed his magic to thread through Llias' soul, but apparently he was not.

"I swear you have nothing to fear from me, Llias," Lonn said, chastened. He should not have been sneaky with his magic, thinking Llias unaware of it. Of course he was not unaware. He was Lonn's familiar; if anyone were sensitive to the presence of Lonn's magic, it would be him.

"Nothing except being kept as your prisoner," Llias countered. "Although apparently being kept as your sex-slave is also an option." He pushed the picked-over tray away and put his feet up on the polished tabletop. "So why the secrecy? What happens if I let it slip that you think I'm your familiar?"

Lonn frowned. "Do not. There is already too much afoot here that I only half understand. Plots and secrets and deceptions. My mother's prophecies and my father's control of the joined worlds, my brother's children, the witch Illt and her plots, and the flow of crystal energy through it. It is all connected, and you and I are at the heart of it, Llias. The less that is known about you, the safer you are."

"I don't feel very safe," Llias retorted. "I feel like I should be sleeping with a knife under my pillow."

Lonn would have been surprised if Llias were not already doing that, but he didn't say so. He was trying to build up the man's trust in him, although he recognized that he was not doing a very good job of it. An idea came to him, and he got up and rummaged through the drawers of his desk. He found what he wanted and put a small metal key in Llias' hand.

"Maybe that will help," he said. "It's the key to your door."

Llias spun it in his fingers and scowled. Lonn could almost see him weighing his next remark carefully, before deciding against speaking it. Perhaps he did not want to give Lonn ideas. Instead, he gave a curt nod and returned to his room, closing and locking the door behind him. He tested the door, making sure that it was actually locked. Lonn didn't blame him for that.

Lonn let his head fall back with a long sigh, staring up at the ceiling as two additional guards tiptoed past and took up their post on the balcony.

The prince was not doing this right, but it was not all his fault. How did he come to this willful Fryst as his arcane familiar? Why could he not have a cat, like his mother? They might have uncanny yellow eyes, but at least they didn't talk back.

# Threat

The next morning, Lonn rose early to find Llias up before him again. He was out on the wide balcony with Myrun and Varla; Lonn could hear their voices floating through the open archway. He hung back to listen, feeling like an intruder in his own chambers.

*"...guard up, up, up..."*

*"...ouch!"*

*"...told you to keep your guard up..."*

Lonn ghosted into view, taking in the scene before him. Llias and the two women seemed to be having a *tanda* training session, with Llias and Varla coaching Myrun.

Myrun was holding the two sticks, her stance messy and imprecise, while Llias and Varla feigned attacks with whatever they found to hand. Varla held her sheathed sword and Llias had his bow, both swinging at Myrun in slow arcs to force her to defend her space.

Lonn watched the easy camaraderie from inside the room. Llias made friends easily, it seemed, even with the soldiers who were guarding him. If Lonn spoke to Hilde about it, they would stop their familiarity — but what then? Lonn would have Llias' time and attention all to himself, but at the cost of a portion of his happiness, at the cost of leaving him more isolated than he already was.

He would not do it, and he forced his jaw to unclench. They were merely sparring. Lonn had sparred with Llias himself; it meant nothing. Llias was outgoing and charming, of course people warmed to him. Fates, Lonn had warmed to him far more than he expected to, allowing him whatever liberties he liked as long as he did not leave. Lonn was glad for Llias to have friends. He was glad of it, and not jealous at all.

Lonn tore himself away and found Erla waiting in the reception room, her new sky-blue silk scarf neatly hemmed and tidily bound around her hair. He asked her to fetch breakfast for Llias, and she nodded and rushed off with a one-handed curtsy. The girl must have been under orders to inform Darrin when the prince awoke, since his friend arrived a few minutes later.

"Darrin." Lonn sighed, glad to see him. "I need your assistance."

Darrin raised his eyebrows. "What is new, my friend?"

"I know," Lonn said, gripping his shoulder. "I know, you have been a loyal friend, and I will not forget it."

Darrin smiled and grabbed a fruit pastry from Erla's tray as she passed by. "I will not *let* you forget it, hmm?" he said through his mouthful of food.

Lonn was loath to ask his friend for any more favors, but he had few other options. "I must go and discuss Vell with my father," he said, the prospect of an audience with the king casting a dark cloud over his morning. "Llias is in need of clothes, of shoes, of comforts for his room. Could you..."

"Take him shopping?" Darrin interrupted. "I'd be glad to."

Lonn winced and looked down awkwardly, "I would prefer Llias stayed in my rooms..."

"Ahh," Darrin said. "Of course. He's your prisoner."

"He is not—" Lonn started, and then gave up with another sigh.

Darrin was right; until Llias accepted his role with Lonn on Otharn, he *was* Lonn's prisoner. Lonn at least would see that he was a spoiled and pampered prisoner, if that was the best he could hope for.

"I cannot leave him alone," Lonn confessed. "He has already climbed over the balcony, and I fear what more he will do when I turn my back."

Darrin nodded, but a frown marred his face. "Aye, I will do it, Lonn, but do you hear yourself? Llias does not want to stay, why do you force him?"

Lonn set his jaw. "He must stay," he said in a low hiss. "He must. Do not ask me to be without him Darrin, because I will not! He is my familiar and I need him."

Darrin held his hands up, and he did not argue. They were friends, but Lonn still was a prince, and he was used to getting his way. Darrin knew when to push and when to yield, and clearly this was a yielding situation.

"Llias, a word," Lonn called.

Llias strolled over, his *tanda* tucked under his arm and a cup of *kurvorur* in his hand, his face screwed up at the bitter taste of it. He was wearing blue silk pajamas he must have taken from Lonn's room sometime the day before. The rising suns cast their light through the window and the cloth glowed. The overlapping blues of the silk, Llias' skin, his hair, and his deep, deep eyes made Lonn lose his train of thought for a moment.

"Llias," he said, recovering. "You remember Darrin."

Darrin gave a gallant bow, swishing his cape over his shoulder, which drew a smile to Llias' face.

"Darrin Gulna Oxi," he said, with an answering bow. "Of course I remember you."

Lonn soldiered on. "Darrin will keep you company while I am gone today. He will help you find new clothes, shoes, furnishing for your room. Anything you want, Llias. Please make yourself at home. Erla is also at your disposal, to take your messages and run any errands you need."

Llias nodded. "Alright Lonn. I am sure I can amuse myself for the day."

His tone and his body language were reserved, but Lonn felt a jump in his arcane senses that told him Llias was pleased. He enjoyed it for a moment, but he would not be able to leave on such a warm note. He could not risk leaving and coming back to an empty room. Not again.

"Llias, one last thing. You are not to leave these rooms."

Llias rolled his eyes. "I know, or there'll be consequences. You already told me."

Lonn ground his teeth. He needed Llias to take his warning seriously, for his own safety as well as Lonn's peace of mind. Lonn would not be able to hurt him; he could not threaten him with any such punishment as a true slave might expect. Beatings, starvation, the lash — he would not do any of that to Llias, and the man clearly knew it. But Llias could still be punished, and his growing friendship with Lonn's guards gave him an idea.

"Llias," he said, forcing the words out through gritted teeth, "if you set one foot outside the door, every one of my guards who allowed it will be given one hundred lashes."

Llias paled. "You wouldn't do that," he said, his eyes flicking to the balcony where Varla and Myrun stood, pretending that they had not heard their prince's threat.

"I will do what is necessary to keep you safe," Lonn said. "Do not test me."

Lonn hid his reaction as all the warmth drained away from him, just as the color had drained from Llias' face. He was hardly proud of making such a threat, and he prayed to the fates that Llias would heed him and not force him to carry it out.

# Covl

Lonn had to face his father, and he wanted to get it over with. It was best to do it early, before the matters of the day had worn him down and soured his temper, although the king's temper was a slender thread at the best of times. Covl was accustomed to obedience, and when he didn't get it, his reaction could be unpredictable. After everything that had happened these past years, and everything that had happened behind his back these past few weeks, Lonn was disinclined to be obedient.

The king's power rose as Lonn headed towards the royal quarters, threads and swirls brushing past him as he walked. Unlike Lonn's own magic, which came when he called, the king *lived* in his power. He swam in it like a fish, he flew in it like a bird. It was as natural to him as breathing, and Lonn wondered if it would be like that for him when Llias eventually embraced their bond. Would he be as powerful as Covl? There was something both thrilling and forbidden about that idea — that such a thing was even possible.

Endless stone hallways gave way to the public rooms of the royal quarters: the library, the solar, spacious reception rooms and broad balconies that captured the morning light, overlooking the city and the forest beyond. Lonn's father was not there, and Lonn had not expected him to be. He would be on the upper floor, in the observatory.

Wards tingled on Lonn's skin as he passed, subtle at first and then increasingly aggressive. Unwelcome visitors would find it impossible to walk these halls. They would be turned around and sent back on their way, confused and disoriented. If they should be strong enough to get past the kind outer wards, the spiral staircase up to the roof had wards far less kind — fire and blade and poison. Lonn shivered as he walked, the power of the defensive spells probing him and allowing him to pass.

The observatory was on the highest floor of the tower. It was a rooftop with a low wall, open to the skies. It was not an observatory of the heavens, although at night the view of the Otharnian sky was spectacular; it was an observatory of the worlds. The low wall was inset with shards of crystal shaped and ground into magnifying lenses, each one focused on a world or person the king considered worthy of his attention.

Lonn looked around, familiar with this place. The king had shown him the worlds here when he was a boy. He had shown his son many and varied treasures, natural wonders, the traditions of his people, their celebrations and tragedies. Lonn felt the weight of his responsibilities here more than anywhere else, more even than in the vast throne room. This was where the king could come and truly understand the scope and scale of his reach. Lonn found it humbling, but he did not know how his father found it.

By the entranceway was a row of crystal lenses set apart from the rest. Two whole and glowing, one smashed to splinters. Those three lenses used to show the king's family: Anlira, Lonn, and Vell. When he was younger, Lonn had been filled with pride that his father should dedicate one of his precious lenses to him, and more than the lens, the gift of his attention. It was thrilling to know that any moment during Lonn's lessons or training or games, his father might glance over to that lens and see him. Now, the lens represented something else; not comfort, but surveillance. Lonn was only able to relax in the carefully warded space of his own chambers.

Lonn and his father had never spoken of the broken lens. It had been whole before Vell was sent to Vaaladir, and Lonn assumed that his father had not liked to face what he had done to his younger son. Lonn looked away from it, avoiding the emotion it churned up in him. He had not come here to fight.

The king had not acknowledged Lonn's arrival, although it was impossible that he should be unaware of it. He was staring into his lenses, his attention flickering between a dozen of them, striding across the observatory, as strong and tall and broad as ever despite his white hair and beard.

"Father," Lonn said, calling his attention with a respectful bow. "I hope you are well."

Covl stopped his pacing and glowered at him. "I am as well as you see me," he growled, impatient. "You have seen your mother? I will speak with you about Vell."

"First, I would make my report about the situation on Tornatt," Lonn tried, but the king waved his words away.

"I am well aware of what you have done on Tornatt," he said, pointing at the crystal lens that showed Lonn even at this moment observing him. "You have brought peace and justice. You have pacified the raiders and secured the vaults. You have shown the power of Otharn to those who would threaten it. And you have returned with a Fryst whore as your prize. Do not make a fool of yourself with him, Lonn, not more than you already have done!"

Lonn held his breath, forcing himself not to react to his father's harsh words. He even ignored the insult to Llias, knowing it was better his father thought *that* of him than anything else. The king was displeased, that much was obvious. Lonn mentally braced himself.

"And while you were gone seeking your glory, your br—the *slave* Vell and his owner have escaped to spawn another monster in secret and in disgrace!"

Lonn swallowed, pushing down the unfairness behind his father dismissing his mission to Tornatt as "glory seeking." He had gone to defend their ally. He had gone to do his duty, not for his own benefit. But it mattered not, and his father would not welcome his disagreement.

"I have heard what happened with Vell and David," he said instead. "Why did you not wait for my return?"

Again, Covl growled at him, pacing the circular observatory, the crystal lenses flaring and sparking as he passed.

"I could not wait," he declared, as though daring Lonn to question him. "Their wards wavered, and I saw at once what they had been trying to hide from me. That human, David Thomen, has been using Vell in the basest ways. He has impregnated him with his seed and another mongrel creature grows in his belly."

"The basest ways?" Lonn shot back, unable to help himself. "What of the Vaaladir? What of their uses, which I saw with my own eyes?" He pointed to the broken shards of Vell's lens. "Do not tell me you did not know. For two years your wards turned me away from this place!"

"The Vaaladir assured me he would not conceive," the king said, biting off the 't' sound of his words as he did when he was getting angry. "It was his rightful punishment. He would have submitted eventually, he would have confessed the location of that wretched beast he called Jormuna, and he could have come home. Now *two* monsters will walk the surface of the joined worlds, I know not where, and they will bring destruction and despair in their wake!"

The two men, king and prince, stared at each other, breathing hard, tempers high. Neither of them wanted to fight, but the peace between them was too fragile. It depended on silence and the denial of unspoken past deeds which would not stay buried. The king let out a long breath and reined in his power, the prickling on Lonn's skin diminishing.

"They have some power, the two of them," Covl said, calmer and back in control of himself. "They defeated Lady Illt and her mages, and they escaped the city using the *fjarleoth*. Vell knows many secret places on this world and others; he is cunning, sly, secretive and he always was that way. Many times in his youth I found my sight of him clouded." He looked over at the broken lens again, next to the lens showing Anlira at her harp.

At the mention of Illt's name, Lonn looked up. Illt was one of the reasons he had brought Llias back to Otharn. He had meant to enlist his parents' help to break Illt's oath, but this did not seem a good time to ask. Lonn had yet to get a measure of the king's mood, and Darrin's message to him echoed in his ears. *Was* the king in his right mind? Covl seemed determined to find Vell. He was focused and single-minded, but had he crossed the line into obsession?

Lonn's silent contemplation was ignored by the king, whose gaze roamed over his lenses, jumping from one to the next without pause. They were all focused on Otharn itself. *He is seeking Vell here,* Lonn realized with a chill.

"Change is coming," Covl said, matter-of-factly. "Fate has turned its eyes to you, Lonn. You are the one who must take action now. I have protected the joined worlds for many long years, but I failed in the matter of Vell's children. I could not avert the prophecy, and so that burden falls to you. The signs could not be clearer. You must find the two monsters and slay them. If you do not, the joined worlds will be rendered apart, and nothing but chaos will rule for generations. You know all this. Your mother has seen it."

Lonn tried to evade the command. "I do not know where they are," he said, but his father exploded.

"Of course you do not; no one does! That is what you must discover, Lonn. You may like to play the fool, but I know you are not one. You are as deep in this as any one of us. Your friend Darrin-with-no-axe aided them. I would have executed him for that crime, but your mother cautioned me not to. He knows more than he will tell any torturer, but he will tell *you,* his dearest friend. He thinks himself well punished now; he did not enjoy his trip to the whipping post and he is no longer a warrior, but the only reason he still draws breath is that you might make use of him to find your brother."

"Darrin had my token!" Lonn exclaimed, furious at his father's words and no longer able to hold back. "He acted on my request, and I return to find you have had him punished like a common criminal!"

*He sold your brother as a slave,* Lonn reminded himself, his chest almost bursting with rage. *There is little he would not do.*

Covl waved his hand, dismissing the matter. "Your mother has seen the destruction of the joined worlds. She has seen the crystal realm shattered and broken by the power of these creatures. There is nothing more critical than preventing that fate, Lonn. Nothing. Billions will die, and you complain of one man's well-deserved punishment. This is what it means to be king. It is a heavy burden."

Lonn held his tongue with great effort. There was nothing more he could say that would not further provoke the king's wrath. They stood side by side for a time, letting the air settle between them, the king's power returning to its usual strong current. In the lenses before them, they watched the city square prepare for Kalkis. Workers set up glittering crystal hangings and decorated the square with winter flowers.

Eventually, Covl grunted.

"When we were younger," he said, "Your mother and I would go to the Kalkis Festival. We would leave you and your brother with the nursemaids and put on our masks and dance in the square." He smiled at the memory, his stern, lined face transformed. It was something Lonn rarely saw: his father as the man, not the king. "We have not done it for years now."

"Perhaps you should," Lonn ventured. "I am sure Mother would enjoy it."

Kalkis was a masked festival, a rare chance for everyone to be equal, anonymous and unobserved. Lonn had always enjoyed it, mingling with his people without a care for rank.

The king frowned, his majestic mask already back in place. "I have no time for such things. And your mother will not leave her garden. Fate is closing in, and she desires always to be open to its warnings."

Covl turned to Lonn and put both hands on his shoulders, gripping him tightly and holding him in place.

"Prince Lonn of Otharn," he said formally, "I know you do not welcome this task, and so I will relieve you of the burden of choice. I charge you with this duty. Put an end to your brother's children and ensure there will be no more. Do not let their power break the joined worlds apart. Kill them first."

Lonn gasped as the king's power flowed into him, seeking to bind him to this duty as surely as Lady Illt had bound him to her bargain. Covl had never done this before to the prince, but Lonn had seen it done to others, willingly — or so Lonn had thought.

Lonn tried to pull free, but his father's grip was too strong, his hands like claws on his shoulders.

"No!" Lonn cried desperately, the binding worming its way under his skin. "No, I won't!"

"You will!" Covl snarled. "Do not fight me, boy, it is easier this way. You can blame me; you can tell all that you had no choice!"

Lonn's arm ached and burned where Illt's oath had burrowed into his flesh as Covl's binding tried to take its place.

"Father!" Lonn cried, pain tearing up his arm, his bones creaking under the strain of it. "Stop, please!"

His bond with Llias flared despite the distance between them, fighting the king's binding, protecting Lonn's arm from shattering under the onslaught. Llias' shock and surprise echoed through the open channel, and Lonn was impossibly grateful that he did not reject the bond at that moment. Instead, he seemed to embrace it, to steady and stabilize it, lending Lonn his strength, giving him a solid foundation to push against. Lonn gathered his power and shoved the king's hands away, severing the attempted binding. They both fell back, off balance. The king kept his feet, but Lonn tripped and dropped to the floor, his arm throbbing with pain, his stomach churning with horror at what his father had tried to do to him.

"I will not kill children!" Lonn swore. "I will not!"

"What is that power?" Covl demanded, staring at Lonn, white-faced and furious. "That will allow you to defy your king?"

"It is me!" Lonn shouted, rolling back to his feet, equally furious and terrified for Llias, for his brother, for the children he was uncle to.

"It is me! I am not your tool; I am not your weapon to be wielded as you please. I am the future King of Otharn and of the joined worlds, and I will not be bound to your duty like a beast to the plow."

They stared at each other, the very air seeming to hold its breath, the flagstones under Lonn's feet as slippery as ice. One wrong step at this moment could doom him and those he cared about. Covl was on the verge of making a decision he would regret, and Lonn could not let that happen.

"I will give you this oath, willingly," Lonn said, taking a deep breath, his mind working overtime. Illt's oath-magic had saved him from the king's binding, but it would not have done so if they were not at odds. There must be some conflict that Lonn had not seen yet. "I will not let the bonds between the worlds break. I will not let the crystal realm shatter. I swear it by my own life."

Covl sneered. "You are a fool. Your oath will bring you to the same action as mine, only this time the choice will be yours, and the blame will be yours too. Be gone from my sight, boy."

# Steam

Lonn was in no mood to return to his chambers. He needed to think, and he did not want his dark mood to affect Llias. His feet took him to the training grounds, and he was about to demand someone to spar with him when he remembered what had happened on Tornatt. The uncontrollable surge of power, the overwhelming battle-fever, the berserker rage that had only been curbed by Llias tackling him to the ground and draining the power out of him.

Shivering at the memory, Lonn realized that sparring was a bad idea. He paced the training grounds, fidgety and anxious, his hands opening and closing into fists. He was collecting questioning looks from those busy training, wondering why the prince was not joining them. He was a frequent visitor to the training grounds, usually with Darrin or the members of his guard.

The encounter with his father hung over his head like a dark cloud. The king had tried to bind him to a duty to kill his brother's children, and only Llias' strength had prevented it. Lonn was appalled that his own father would do that to him, and then he was appalled at his own naiveté to think that Covl *wouldn't*. His thoughts spiraled around on themselves like a snake eating its tail.

He paced the soft ground, the familiar sounds surrounding him: the clash of metal on metal, the *thunk* of wood on wood, the shouts and grunts and cheers of the competitors. Lonn had hoped the well-known place would calm his thoughts, but it was having the opposite effect because he could not join in. He did not dare do it without Llias.

Unconsciously, he reached out through the bond to find his familiar, checking that the connection was still there. It was, and a quick pulse answered his inquiry, carrying with it a hint of Llias' questioning uncertainty, which was unsurprising after the brutal encounter with Covl's magic. Lonn rocked on his heels as he sent back reassurance. Even that small taste of a willing connection was a heady feeling, instantly chasing away his moody pondering. As though conjured into his mind, Lonn could almost feel Llias' blue hands on him, and the rush of power like the bubbles of *ampavin* wine popping under his skin. The sensation was arousing and intimate, and like nothing Lonn had ever felt before. The temperature at training grounds increased, and Lonn's clothes suddenly were too restrictive and tight on his body.

Lonn turned on his heel and headed for the baths at a brisk pace, his mind turned in an entirely different direction. He found an unoccupied steam room and locked the door behind him, stripping off his clothes and tossing them toward the bench, letting them fall onto the floor without care. He tipped a ladle of water and a sprinkle of fragrant dried herbs on the hot crystals in the center of the room and let out a long sigh. Haze drifted through the dim light, and the soft hiss and pop of the hot crystals was the only sound.

*Llias.* Lonn reached out again, but this time Llias only allowed it for a moment. No doubt he could sense that Lonn was in no danger, and was merely curious and seeking his attention. Llias sent another pulse back to Lonn, this one of exasperation and impatience, and then he cut the connection.

Lonn smiled at his willful Fryst. Llias did not make it easy, but Lonn found he liked him that way. Nearly every person Lonn met had an ulterior motive to be pleasant to him, to accommodate him, to please him. But not Llias. For the first time, Lonn had to work for someone's affection, to flex emotional muscles he had never realized he had, and he found that he did not mind it as much as he expected. Some things were worth working for.

He hoped that Llias was enjoying himself, that Darrin was entertaining him and showing him the many benefits of his new life. For one thing, Lonn had a virtually unlimited budget and Llias could spend it as he liked. Lonn was sure Darrin was helping him do that right at that moment.

In the locked steam room, and with the connection to Llias firmly cut, Lonn considered it safe to indulge himself a little. He stretched out on the bench, bringing Llias back to his mind. His smile; white teeth against blue skin. His deep eyes, reflective as dark mirrors, the glossy blue of his hair. And more than that, more than his appearance, although Lonn did not deny that was pleasant enough, was his spirit. His strength, his refusal to give up and submit. As frustrating as Lonn found it, he also admired it.

A quiet sigh passed Lonn's lips, sweat prickling his skin, his eyes falling closed, the fantasy too enticing to resist. Perhaps one day Llias would willingly indulge him. Lonn rubbed his hands down his chest, his flat belly, his hips, the insides of his thighs, eyes closed, imagining Llias doing the same, picturing him sitting astride his lap, his blue skin flushed to violet, his hands touching Lonn's body, teasing, drawing out his power, playing with it, letting it twine around his fingers and sink back into Lonn's flesh. Lonn panted, licked his lips, and let the fantasy float away. Instead, he visualized his familiar just as he was: Llias on the archery range, his form precise and perfect, or in the training ring, holding his *tanda* at guard position, fierce determination on his face.

Lonn reached down and gave himself one long stroke. He was already aroused, and that single touch was almost too much for his sensitive flesh. He had no right to do it, but he imagined Llias in the room with him — not as a teasing fantasy, but as he probably would be. Challenging, insubordinate, demanding. He would not even touch Lonn if he were there; he would just watch him with his midnight eyes. He would sit there fully dressed, and look Lonn over from head to toe, judging him. Lonn stroked himself again at the thought, harder this time.

Lonn knew he was handsome. He possessed many mirrors, and he was not prone to self-delusion, but the thought of Llias' appraising gaze sent him a delicious thrill through him. Would Llias like what he saw? Would he want to see more? Lonn bit his lip, working himself in earnest now, his eyes falling closed, his mental image replaced only by sensation, by the physical and the arcane growing closer at every moment. The heated crystals glowed and glimmered, pulsing with the overspill of Lonn's power. Energy flowed through him, his every cell alight with it, bursting with it, desperate not just for his climax but to join with his familiar, to share his spirit, his soul, his heart.

Lonn gasped and blinked, shocked at the sudden rush and eager arrival of his orgasm. Just like his arcane power, his other energies seemed invigorated by Llias' presence as well. Lonn lay there, unwilling to move, enjoying his afterglow and the memory of deep blue eyes.

The heat made him drowsy, languid and content after his climax. He would stay for a while, let the heat and steam relax him, and give Llias time to enjoy the rest of his morning. The hard bench under him was not a concern at all. Lonn was a soldier, as well as a prince, and he was used to rough conditions. He put one arm under his head and closed his eyes.

***

It was cold, freezing cold, when Lonn opened his eyes again. The steam room was lined with ice, sparkling in the light from crystals that were no longer red hot but frozen blue. Lonn scrambled up, the bench icy under him, tearing at his skin as he ripped himself from it. He rubbed his eyes, the room wavering in his vision, the edges fading to black. The towel was gone, his clothes, gone. His breath hung in the air, the clouds of vapor the only movement in the utter silence of the room. Lonn lunged at the door, but it was coated in a thick layer of ice and sealed shut. Lonn hammered on it, but the thuds were dull, the sound absorbed by the chill, heavy air.

*"Have you made up your mind, Prince?"*

Lonn spun, already knowing whom he would see. The shadowy cloaked figure of Illt, standing opposite the glowing crystals. Her heavy cloak once again shadowed her injured face, and only the glint of her teeth showed under her hood. Lonn opened his hand to summon Skarpur, but nothing happened. His power did not answer; the spear that had been his constant companion since he'd come of age was concealed from him, as though it had never been.

Lonn relaxed. This was a dream, then. There was no power in all the joined worlds that could keep him apart from Skarpur. His father had told him that when he presented it to him, and Lonn knew it was true. When all else failed, when all was lost and the worlds themselves destroyed, even then the spear would answer his call. Their bond was forged in blood, Lonn's blood, the blood of his father, of his forbears. Every one of his ancestors who had wielded the spear would bend the fates from the afterlife to return Skarpur to the one who owned it. The bond grew stronger with every generation, and when Lonn gave the spear to his own successor, it would grow stronger still. Skarpur did not answer, therefore this was a dream.

Lonn folded his arms, heedless of his nudity, and faced Illt's shade.

"What do you want?" he demanded.

"You are enjoying your slave's company?" Illt inquired with a giggle, gesturing at Lonn's crotch. "He has not yet succumbed to your charm, that you must entertain yourself alone?"

"*What* do you *want*?" Lonn repeated, making a heroic effort to keep his tone even. Illt was dangerous, always, always dangerous, and the more playful she seemed the worse her intent. She played with her prey like a cat with a mouse. Lonn had seen her do it.

Illt shrugged, tossed her head as though her long blonde braid were still there, floating in the invisible currents of her power.

"I felt the twisting of your oath, Prince," she said, "Do not try anything clever. Clever doesn't suit you, and it never has. Remember the price you will pay if you disappoint me."

"It has been one day," Lonn said, impatient with the witch. "Do you think I can return to Otharn and track down my brother, whom the king himself cannot scry, and get you your prize in a single day?"

Illt laughed. "So, even the king cannot find that little *elskan*? He has shut down the *fjarleoth* in the city for days now, trying to trace him, but I am not surprised that he fails. He allowed blind-spots to fester under his very nose. He lectured me on the virtues of balance and judgment...He is an old fool. Do not follow in his footsteps."

"Why do you want the children?" Lonn demanded. "The king banished you, cast you aside like worthless trash. Surely you do not still do his bidding, chase his approval? What is your purpose?"

Illt snarled, the eerie blue light from the crystals glinting on her bared teeth under her hood. "Just bring them to me alive."

"Alive?" Lonn said, still trying to understand the purpose behind her demand and comparing it to the binding his father had tried to force on him. "My father wants them dead, but you want them alive — why?"

"Do not try to understand things that do not concern you, Prince," Illt said. All traces of her playful humor were gone now, replaced by the malignant spite that was its inverse. "If you do not bring me the children, your precious slave will be mine, and I will take his power, just as I did with the *hafmeyja* and *einhyrnn*!"

Lonn stared at her, horrified, and she cackled. "Oh, yes. He is a creature of magic, just as they were, and as your bond grows so too does his well of power. If you fail to bring me those monsters, I will take him to my altar!"

Lonn lurched toward her, hands outstretched to clasp her throat, but he fell through her and awoke as he tumbled onto the floor of the steam room, eyes wide, heart pounding, panting for breath.

# Dinner

Lonn hurried back to his rooms as a brisk march, holding himself back from running by force of will alone. His heart was in his throat, and he desperately needed to see Llias and ensure he was unharmed — although he was in one of the safest places in the palace, guarded by elite troops, and if anything happened to him, Lonn would know it at once through their bond. Lonn turned the corner to his quarters and blinked at the veritable parade coming out of his rooms. There were servants carrying bundles and baskets, following well-dressed merchants. After them came palace housekeepers carrying platters and dishes.

Lonn had never had so many people in his quarters in his life. He preferred to never entertain in his rooms. The interlopers all bowed as they passed him and behaved respectfully enough, so Lonn pushed down his irritation. He had told Darrin to entertain Llias, and his friend evidently had.

Ake and Nife were back on duty and stood by the door as the parade went by them, looking ahead and not moving a muscle. Lonn paused.

"Is all well, Sergeant Ake?" he asked.

Ake nodded, "Aye, my prince. Llias...that is...your guest... has had many visitors, and young Erla's feet have hardly touched the ground all day, but all is well."

Lonn smiled, tension falling away from him at the scene. Of course Llias was safe here, and he seemed to have enjoyed himself as well. Lonn noted Ake's hesitation over Llias' name. He would have to think of how he wanted others to address his new companion. Llias seemed happy to go by his first name, and his guard had little idea what to make of his role and status. That was something for another day, though.

Entering the room, Lonn found Darrin and Llias on the balcony, looking out over the city while the last housekeepers set the living room back to rights. For some reason, a large black raven perched on the railing next to the two men, allowing Darrin to cautiously stroke its glossy head. Lonn had never seen a wild raven so close before, or so fearless. He moved to join them.

Llias turned at his approach, and the raven startled and took off, circling the balcony before swooping down over the city and vanishing. Llias watched it go, then leaned back against the balustrade, the suns on his face. He was wearing new clothes, tailored to his size, a simple white shirt and dark-blue pants. It was nothing elaborate, but the difference between his new attire and Lonn's borrowed, ill-fitting clothes shoved all other thoughts out of Lonn's mind. When he leaned back a little further, a tiny sliver of skin showed above his waistband that made Lonn clench his fist behind his back.

Darrin gave Lonn a knowing smile, patted him on the shoulder and pointed to the stack of bills he had left on his desk under the *halfor* statue.

"I will take my leave," he said, "I am sure you two have much to discuss."

Lonn thanked him distractedly, transfixed by the sight of Llias at his ease, wearing clean and well-fitting clothes.

"Greetings, Llias," Lonn said, unsure where to put his hands. He clasped them behind his back again, which was overly formal, but the alternative would be to grin like a fool and bathe in the pleasure of his arcane energy coming back to its home.

"Greetings, Lonn," Llias replied, waving one hand, his elbows on the railing behind him. "I'm still here, as you see. No one needs to be whipped."

"Indeed, you are still here, and I am very glad to see you." Llias' pointed remark could not dull Lonn's pleasure in his company, and he leaned on the wall opposite. He hoped to spend some time with his familiar, to bask in his presence.

Before he could think of what to say next, there was a crash behind them and Erla tumbled through the inner door, an ornate lute carried carefully in her arms. She was talking as she entered, excited to deliver her burden, but stopped short when she saw Lonn. She bowed and greeted him formally, her easy smile gone. "My prince," she said, "I beg your pardon, I have this...excuse me..."

Llias rescued her. "Thank you, Erla. Just put it in my room with the rest."

Erla blushed and bowed again, then hurried to Llias' room to leave the instrument.

"You play?" Lonn asked, desiring nothing more than to have Llias perform for him and enjoy some peaceful music.

Llias gave him a hard look. "I do," he said, "for my friends."

Lonn ground his teeth. He deserved that, he supposed, but still it stung, especially after their connection earlier in the day and his steam-room fantasy. On a whim, he said, "We will eat here tonight, on the balcony."

Llias looked as though he would prefer not to, but in the end he nodded. Lonn was delighted. When Erla came out of Llias' room, Lonn told her to fetch dinner for them both in an hour. Erla curtsied her agreement, declined to look Lonn in the eye, and scurried out.

"What has gotten into her?" Lonn asked.

"We-e-ell," Llias said, drawing out the word, "she was standing right there when you threatened to whip your guards if I left your rooms. I'm sure she's not forgotten about that. What are you going to do to *her* if I displease you?"

Lonn swallowed his objection. Llias was not wrong, and although Lonn could claim he would not harm the girl, Llias had no reason to believe him. He had already threatened the only other people Llias knew on this entire world. Lonn was not doing anything right, and he felt like every step he made was the wrong one. He decided to retreat before he did anything else to upset his familiar.

"I will bathe and change before dinner," he said. Telling himself he was not running away, he went to his bedroom.

He did bathe and change, into softer clothes than his usual multi-layered daytime attire. That took less than ten minutes, and Lonn wondered if he should go back out and try to talk with Llias or let him have some time to himself. He ended up just pacing the room, increasing his anxiety with every minute.

Needless to say, the hour passed excruciating slowly.

When he finally emerged, Lonn found the table set out on the balcony, shaded lamps and soft cushions decorating the space. He sent Myrun and Varla out to the hallway and made a mental note to do something nice for Erla. Maybe he should reassure her that he would not punish her for anything that Llias did. She really was a good page, and Lonn wondered why he had put off getting one for so long.

Llias joined him a few minutes after the hour, and they sat on opposite sides of the table. In the purple glow of Foubla setting, and with the shaded lamp lighting his face from below, Llias looked like a creature of magic. He looked wondrous. Lonn's skin tingled as he poured Llias a glass of wine and his magic twined itself around him. Lonn smiled, his wine in his hand, relishing the moment. This is what he could be enjoying all the time, if only Llias would cease his resistance.

"Tell me of your day, Llias" Lonn asked, looking forward to hearing of Llias' enjoyment of his generosity.

Llias tore apart a piece of fresh bread with his fingers. "Actually," he said, putting an end to Lonn's daydream as easily as he put an end to the bread, "I'd rather talk about *your* day. What happened? Did someone attack you? I felt it from here, like something tearing at you, pulling you away, trying to...*change* you somehow. What was that? Was it the witch?"

Lonn drained his wine and poured himself another cup. "That was my father," he said shortly, his good mood evaporated.

Llias raised his eyebrows, chewed and swallowed the bread he was eating. "Go on," he said, his deep eyes fixed on Lonn, refusing to take his clear hint that the prince did not want to discuss it.

With a sigh, Lonn gave in. He could hardly keep secrets from his familiar, not when it was his allowance of their bond that had saved him. He explained what had happened; the only detail he could not reveal was the oath that he had given to Illt. Everything else, he told.

"Huh," Llias said when he was done. "So your father is an asshole?"

Lonn choked on his wine.

"Sorry," Llias said, holding up his hand. "I meant to say a *controlling* asshole."

"My father is the king of Otharn and guardian of the joined worlds!" Lonn sputtered, dabbing at his wine-drenched shirt with a napkin.

Llias nodded. "Uh-huh," he said. "And he thinks of you as...what? A little *kas* game piece that he can move on the board wherever he wants?"

Lonn stared at Llias, shocked at the words coming from his mouth, even though a part of him recognized their veracity. That was exactly what his father had tried to do, and Llias had stopped him from doing it.

"It is not like that," Lonn muttered, "He is the king. He has many cares, many responsibilities."

"Of course, he does," Llias agreed easily. "Just as you do. You are your father's *kas*-piece and I am yours, no? He wants you to obey him, and you want me to obey you. It makes sense to me now, why you are the way you are."

Lonn drank another cup of wine. He could not even deny it. He *did* want and expect Llias' obedience, because he was the crown prince and Llias was his arcane familiar. He was Lonn's, and his obedience was Lonn's right. *Your father is the king,* a treacherous thought whispered in his ear, *your obedience is* his *right, and you do not give it.* Lonn's jaw ached, Llias' eyes on him, their dark depths reflecting the light of the lamp. He did not speak, merely waited for Lonn to acknowledge the truth of what he had said, or to lie and deny it.

"Thank you for helping me," Lonn said instead. "I know you did not have to do that, to allow the connection to remain strong. But I would not have been able to resist the bond without you, so thank you."

Llias nodded. "I did not think too hard on it," he confessed. "Just as when I halted your berserker rage at the camp. It is not in my interest to encourage harm to come to you while I am trapped here at your mercy. Though take note, Lonn, this is the second time I have aided you. The goodwill of your prisoner will not last forever."

It might be true, but still Llias' cold-hearted response left Lonn disappointed. He had hoped Llias was warming to him, but it seemed the barrier to their situation remained, and as far as Llias was concerned, it was insurmountable. Lonn's fingers tightened on his cup, knuckles white. *How long would this go on?*

"You are only a prisoner as long as you refuse to accept your role here," he said, trying to be patient with Llias' intransigence.

"No," Llias retorted, drumming his fingers on the wood of the table. "I am a prisoner for as long as you refuse to let me leave."

"Do not argue with me!" Lonn growled, their pleasant dinner ruined. All his efforts to keep his familiar happy came back around to the same argument that Llias would not give up.

"I will argue with you as much as you deserve," Llias shot back. "I will argue with you every cursed day you keep me here against my will."

"Why do you even want to leave?" Lonn demanded. "Why do you want to return to that frozen world? What is there for you that can compare to this?"

He gestured to the palace, the city, the glory of the night sky, taking in everything that surrounded them, every comfort and luxury that he could provide if only Llias would accept it.

Llias snarled at him. He shoved back from the table and paced the balcony before he replied. "I am *ishaxha*," he said. "I have told you that many times, and you have never once asked me what it means. I have told you that my people need me, and you do not even know why. You ask me why I must leave? Well, there is your answer! I must leave because you do not care about me, you do not care about my people, you do not care about my world. You only care about what I can do for you. Do not deny it, Lonn. It is the truth."

Lonn stared at Llias, at his fury in the lamplight, the waves of his anger flowing through their connection, breaking against Lonn like storm-tossed waves against a rocky shore. Out of instinct, Lonn reached through the bond and tugged on it, just as Llias had done to him back on Tornatt. He wanted Llias to feel their connection, to understand why he had to stay on Otharn with Lonn, but the reaction was not at all what he desired.

Llias severed the connection with a sharp cut of his hand. "Don't you dare!" he hissed, outraged, "Don't you dare try to enforce your will on me. You are no better than your father!"

"I wasn't trying to..." Lonn protested, but the damage was done. Lonn flinched as Llias' door slammed behind him, and the key turned in the lock.

# Orange Blossom at Night

Llias lay on the bed and scowled up at the ceiling, his hands folded behind his head. Every day he thought that he was on the verge of changing his situation with Lonn, but he always ended up back in the same place. Nothing he had yet done had made Lonn realize the futility of forcing him to stay on Otharn. Llias had fought him, he had run away from him, he had reasoned with him. He had even saved Lonn twice: once from his own lack of control, and once from the King of Otharn himself!

If that did not persuade Lonn to respect him as an individual and an equal, Llias had little idea what would.

It was infuriating that Llias could not simply hate his captor and be done with it. It certainly would make things a lot easier. Llias was armed now, and Lonn let his guard down around him so frequently that Llias wanted to throttle him for his foolishness. How could he have such trust in the man he was holding against his will?

But despite everything the prince had done, Llias did not hate Lonn. He could not, no matter how much he wanted to, because Lonn was right: They were connected. They shared a magical bond unlike anything Llias had ever experienced.

He had denied it at first. He had refused to recognize the constant tingle on his skin that was Lonn's magic wrapping around him. He had dismissed the attraction he felt, denied the arcane force that acted on some under-layer of his brain like the scent of orange blossom. Still, it pulled him in, drew him close and buried itself in his brain so deeply that it never went away. The moment he relaxed his vigilance, the intoxicating scent floated by on the breeze and Llias was lured back.

Worse, Llias could not even deny that he liked Lonn. The prince was friendly and charming, and he seemed intent on being honest. He had allowed Llias to arm himself, he had introduced him to his friend Darrin, who seemed to have a good heart. The only problem was that

Lonn had a ridiculous, stubborn, blind spot with this prisoner nonsense, and Llias could not make him see it.

The question Lonn had asked him preyed on Llias' mind: why did he want to leave? What was on Fryst for him to return to? His answer to Lonn had been only half the truth. He was angry with the selfish prince for all the reasons he had stated, but in his heart, he knew that all that waited for him on Fryst was his duty. Travelling alone from place to place, often far from the cities, working his powers on the volcanic waters that kept his world alive. He had friends, to be sure, people who would open their doors to him as he travelled, share a meal or a night or two, and then he would be on his way again. There was no one there who wanted him the way Lonn did. No one so desperate to keep him close. The closest he had to a home on Fryst was the temple, and even there his duty bound him. His welcome was not unconditional, the way it seemed to be with Lonn.

Llias held up his hands and concentrated on the tingling sensation. He was no mage, no sorcerer; the power of ishaxha did not come from the crystal realm, it came from Fryst itself. It was power called from the volcanic core of that world; a power of heat and the flow of water, a power of ice and balance. It was nothing like Lonn's magic, which was energy in the rawest form.

Llias focused. The touch of Lonn's power was light as a feather at the moment. Llias had shoved it away from himself in frustration at Lonn's stubbornness, but as always it had found its way back. Llias doubted Lonn was doing it consciously. Lonn was clumsy when he used his power, seeming to barely understand it himself. When he had tried to pull at Llias through their bond, it had been like a cat clawing at his leg, determined but easily removed.

It had not been like that earlier that day, when Lonn's father had struck at him. The link had slammed open like a floodgate bursting, and Llias had been plunged headfirst into Lonn's pain, his desperation, his urgent need. He had responded instinctively, ignoring the merchants and Darrin in the room with him. He had caught Lonn's untamed power, holding it and steadying it, controlling the flow just as he did with the heated waters of Fryst. He had turned the rampaging flood into a single, powerful wave, and sent it back to Lonn for him to use as he needed.

As he thought about it, a glow formed above his palms. It was not his own power but Lonn's, being pulled through the connection into his hands. Llias could not use it, just as he could not swim in the rivers of Fryst as they emerged scalding hot from the volcanic chambers. He could only shape and direct it. It took only a little focus to pull more power towards him. It was like setting an aqueduct to the correct angle; not too much, and not too little. The energy pulsed in his hands, and Llias raised his head to check his lock was turned before he let it wash over the rest of him too, covering him in a wave of bright, hot sensation.

Llias bit his lip. Lonn was right there in the next room, and he had given Llias every reason to think that he would welcome a knock at his door. It was tempting. It was not only the allure of Lonn himself, although that was a factor, but the allure of knowledge that enticed him. Before him was the possibility of doing something that no ishaxha had ever done: mastering the energy of the crystal realm.

Llias sighed and spun the energy up into a tight ball. He let it pulse back down the connection to Lonn, who probably had no idea what he had even done. If Lonn had as much self-awareness as he had good looks, this would be much easier for everyone. But he did not; the prince was overburdened with one and lacking in the other.

Llias let his eyes drift closed. The tingle of Lonn's magic wrapped around him like a warm blanket, and the scent of orange blossom floated in the air as he went to sleep.

# Sample

Lonn awoke in a good mood. He had slept well, his mind untroubled, and he had a feeling that the day was going to go well. He would do better. He would apologize to Llias for how their dinner had ended, and he would make it up to him. Lonn rose and quickly dressed, for once up and about before Llias, which he took as another good sign. Perhaps Llias had slept well too.

It was early, and the living room was washed in the orange glow of Sinugult's light. Foubla was still below the horizon; the liminal time of the morning grew longer and longer as the Kalkis Festival approached. Generally, the day began only when both suns were in the sky, which made for long, lazy mornings at this time of the year.

Despite that, the palace crafters had already been in the room to install a containment field on the balcony. The flicker of energy was visible in the early light, and Lonn was glad of it. He would tolerate no more escape attempts. His guards had also returned to their usual posts outside the outer door, and Lonn had his private space back.

*Llias will be without company*, he thought to himself. He was guiltily aware of Llias' friendship with the guards, but it only made him more determined to convince Llias to embrace his place here. If he did that, Llias could have more freedom. He could walk through the palace, visit the city with an escort, find friends of his own, enjoy entertainments as he pleased. It was all just waiting for him, but until Lonn could be sure Llias would not try to escape again none of it was possible. Llias was stubborn, and perhaps his anger toward Lonn was somewhat justified, but yesterday had proved that he was aware of the bond between them. He could not reject it forever.

The control device for the containment field lay on the table, and Lonn tossed it into the drawer of his desk before he went to Llias' door.

A melodious tune seeped from under the thick wood of the door, slowly picked out on the lute that Erla had provided the day before.

Lonn listened, captivated, straining to hear more. Llias was a musician, then, as well as an *ishaxha* — whatever that was. No wonder he enjoyed company, no wonder he made friends wherever he went. The music faded away and Lonn raised his hand to tap on the door. A short pause, and Llias opened it, leaning on the stone frame, his arms folded.

"Good morning, Llias," Lonn said, drinking in the sight of the man, his magic swirling inside and around him, eager to find its way to where it longed to be.

Llias nodded. "Lonn," he said, and then nothing more, waiting for Lonn to state his business.

Lonn ground his teeth, took a calming breath, and did what he had come to do. "Llias, I apologize for last night. I should not have tried to use magic on you. My impulse got the better of me."

Llias pressed his lips together, unimpressed. "You need to learn to control yourself then," he said, and Lonn recalled he had said the same thing after his berserker rage on Tornatt.

"I am trying," he said. *It would be a lot easier if you were not so infuriating,* he thought, but he did not say that part out loud. Instead he said, "Would you like to walk with me?"

He hoped that Llias would not decline an invitation to leave his rooms. Llias had been in these same rooms for days now, and today even the guards he had spent time with were gone.

Lonn continued, "We can go to the gardens, or into the city if you like. The decorations for Kalkis are going up; we could eat breakfast in the main square and watch the preparations." Lonn almost bit his tongue in an effort to stop himself from saying more. He was overselling it, trying to persuade Llias to spend time with him like a boy with his first crush. It was not becoming, but still he found himself shuffling his feet awkwardly as Llias considered his answer.

"Very well," Llias said, eventually.

Lonn's heart lifted. He had known this day would go well, and his premonition was turning out to be true. But he did have to remind Llias of how to behave in public.

"Remember, outside of these rooms you must be—"

"Your adoring and accommodating rescued slave," Llias sighed. "Yes, I remember. Do not worry, no one will know you think me your familiar."

Lonn smiled and stepped back, allowing him to pass. Side by side, they headed through the reception room to the outer door where Hilde and Varla were standing.

"Accompany us," Lonn ordered.

The two guards fell in behind them, but before they could leave, Erla appeared at the top of the stairs, her arms full of packages.

Llias smiled at her. "Good morning, Erla! Are those from the tailor?"

"Yes, Llias," she said from behind the bundles, slightly breathless. "And from Lady Kina's jewelers as well." Lonn saw a sizable silk bag hanging from the girl's arm, presumably Llias' purchase from that establishment.

"Wonderful!" Llias said, pleased. "Exactly what I need. I'll just be two minutes. Wait for me here, Lonn." Llias grabbed half the packages from Erla and the two of them vanished into Lonn's rooms, leaving Lonn standing outside.

Lonn scarcely knew what to do with himself. This had literally never happened to him before — to be left waiting for his own companion outside his own rooms. Hilde and Varla stared into the middle-distance, avoiding making any comment or even eye contact with their prince.

*He is testing you after last night,* Lonn told himself. That knowledge and his determination to prove himself made the wait easier to tolerate. Luckily, Llias did not test him too much. He appeared only a few minutes later with his white shirt changed for one of sky-blue silk, perfectly matching the guard's uniforms and Erla's headscarf. Lonn swallowed and cleared his throat, his temper melting away at the sight.

"That is a good color on you, Llias," he said, which was a vast understatement. The sight of his familiar wearing his colors, the sky-blue perfectly setting off the lighter blue of his skin, took Lonn's breath away.

Llias gave him a knowing look but didn't comment. "Let's go then," he said.

"Of course," Lonn replied, the air between them thawing, the comfort and warmth of their connection growing. Lonn even dared to hold out his arm for Llias to take as they walked down the stairs.

"Consider this a free sample," Llias murmured as they walked through the palace arm in arm.

"A sample of what?" Lonn asked, the buzz and thrill of Llias' hand on his arm almost too much for him to process. Even through his jacket and shirtsleeve, it was intoxicating. The pleasure of the touch spread out through his body from that single point of contact.

"A sample of how things could be," Llias said.

"Llias you know I cannot —" Lonn started, but Llias squeezed his arm and shushed him.

"No, I'm not going to argue about it. This is what you're missing out on." Llias walked a little closer, his arm brushing Lonn's side, his sparkling eyes looking up at Lonn adoringly.

Lonn's knees were weak, "Do not tease me," he growled, but he did not pull away. He could not. Already the threads and ribbons of his power were twining around Llias' heart, showing them both their bond and where their power could flow if they would only allow it.

"You deserve it," Llias said with an impudent smile. "You are keeping me locked up as your sex-slave, so I think a little teasing is actually the least you deserve."

"Do not say such things!" Lonn hissed, looking over his shoulder. Hilde and Varla were clearly within earshot, both keeping their faces expressionless, looking ahead.

Llias grinned up at him, and Lonn took another deep breath, one of many such calming breaths he would be taking that day, he could already tell.

They walked down the long, sloped boulevard from the palace as the golden disk of Sinugult climbed in the sky and Foubla's purple light began to spill over the horizon. Lonn told Llias about them as they walked, about Sinugult and Foubla, the two lovers that chased each other endlessly over the sky of Otharn. In turn, Llias told Lonn about the distant blue star of Fryst called Lady Orlane that provided light but little heat. The conversation distracted Lonn from Llias' flirtatious presence at his side, and they reached the main square without incident.

Hilde steered them to a cafe in a quiet corner where Myrun was standing by an empty table, scowling at anyone to dared to sit too close. Lonn was pleased and impressed. He had not even noticed Hilde sending a message to make such preparations. She must have told Erla to run to the guardroom while Lonn got distracted by the sight of Llias in his new shirt.

They sat, and a server brought them hot *kurvorur* and a selection of warm bread. Llias pulled apart the bread, ignoring the *kurvorur*. After a moment, Myrun vanished and came back with a jug of sweet, cold spring water instead, which Llias took with a grateful smile.

The festival preparations were well underway, and the square was a bustle of activity. Not even the king's new restrictions on travel could dampen the city's celebration. Every cafe and store was decorated with sparkling glass, even crystal for those that could afford it. The fountain in the center of the square had been adorned with hundreds of crystal and glass gems, and the sparkling light of the water reflected through them in a riot of rainbow colors. The square would be the focal point of the festivities, and workers put finishing touches on the temporary stages for musicians and performers to use, as well as small booths for soothsayers. Fortune telling was always very popular at the turning points of the year. Wheeled carts sold elaborate masks, with fur and feathers, gems and ribbons adorning each one. After sunset, the revelers would trade masks until no one knew who was who, and then the late night festivities would begin.

Lonn always enjoyed that part; anonymous in his face-paint and mask, he could mingle freely with the crowds, trading masks and kisses and finding pleasurable company until sunrise the next day. Seeing Llias' eye wander to the stalls, Lonn offered to buy him a mask, but Llias declined with a smile.

"It would hardly be fair if you know what my mask will be, Lonn," he said, and Lonn smiled back at him. He would know Llias anywhere, not just by his blue hair and skin, but by the magic that bound them and flowed between them, stronger with every moment.

Despite their discreet corner table, Lonn and Llias were hardly inconspicuous. Lonn's face was well known, and the uniform of his guards even more so. Llias, with his exotic appearance and his sky-blue shirt drew many eyes also, and his behavior — sitting close to Lonn, whispering in his ear, holding his arm — made him appear exactly what Lonn had said he should be: the prince's adoring and grateful rescued slave.

Daring, Lonn squeezed his arm around Llias, encouraging him rest his head on his broad shoulder. Llias allowed it, smiling against Lonn's neck. He whispered into Lonn's ear in a low voice that resonated through Lonn's every nerve, prickling under his skin, sending shivers down his spine.

"Is this not better, Lonn? Would you not rather have me like this, your willing companion, instead of your resentful prisoner?"

"Yes," Lonn admitted honestly. "Yes, Llias, I would much prefer it, of course I would. We are fated to be together. I do not expect you to share my bed, or even to eschew other company, but surely you know it too. You can feel the eyes of fate on us. We must be together."

Llias sighed and sat upright again. He tore off another piece of sweetbread and ate it, offering Lonn a bite from his fingertips.

"Lonn, you must choose," he said, "The eyes of fate mean nothing to me. You can have a prisoner who resents you, or you can have a companion who can come and go as he pleases. Those are the choices. There is no other option. There is no path where you keep me locked up, but I fall into your arms anyway."

Lonn opened his mouth to protest, but Llias kept talking.

"Do not deny it Lonn, I know your desire. I felt it yesterday just as clearly as I feel *this.*" Llias sent a pulse through their link, a single, vibrating burst of energy that rang Lonn's arcane heart like a bell. Llias turned in his chair, pressed against Lonn's side, his blue hand hot on Lonn's thigh, his breath warm in his ear. "Lonn, I do not deny I feel it too, but I swear to you, I will never, ever return your affection if you do not give me my freedom. I swear it by the light of Lady Orlane herself."

Lonn smiled. He was not averse to a challenge, and this side of Llias was one he wanted to encourage — flirtatious, charming, and affectionate. Llias wanted to tease; well, two could play at that game.

"You are missing out, then," he said, running his fingertips down the back of Llias' neck under the open collar of his new shirt, stroking his blue skin.

Llias snorted, but he didn't move away. "Missing out on what? The pleasures of your bedroom? In my experience, rich men care less for their partner's pleasure than poor ones, and handsome men less than either of them."

Lonn seized his opportunity. "So you think me handsome?" he asked, and Llias laughed out loud, his eyes dancing in the reflections of the crystal decorations surrounding them.

"Oh no," he said, straightening his face and pulling away from Lonn to grab the last bread roll on the table. "No, no, no. That was just a general observation. I have a very good idea of what I am missing out on, Lonn, and I have no desire to endure whatever entitled, ill-considered groping you would call seduction."

Lonn waited until Llias looked back at him. "I might surprise you," he said, and held Llias' gaze as he slowly and deliberately licked his lips.

Llias choked on his mouthful of bread, sputtering crumbs as Lonn thumped his back and passed him the cup of water. When Llias looked up again, his face was flushed pale purple, and he could not keep the delighted grin off his face, or stop the wave of sparkling energy that flowed through their bond.

"I did not think noble lords did such things," Llias confessed, wiping the stray crumbs off his shirt.

"I'm the crown prince," Lonn said, leaning back on his chair with another meaningful flick of his tongue over his teeth. "I do whatever I want."

Lonn took another chance and reached through their connection just as Llias had done, sending a sharp, hot pulse through it. It was a taste of his desire, of his passion, of his willingness to indulge Llias in whatever manner he might like to be indulged. The shudder that chased up Llias' spine was all the reaction he wanted. A moment later, Llias recovered and retaliated by sending an icy chill back to Lonn, making him gasp and swig from his hot drink to ward off the cold.

Lonn grinned at him, enjoying this game — this dance that Llias himself had initiated. Perhaps he had not expected Lonn to join in with quite such enthusiasm, but he did not seem to object. In fact, far from objecting, Llias seemed to be enjoying it just as much as Lonn.

# Injury

Llias returned to his room that afternoon, but he left the door open, which Lonn took as a great victory. He was exceedingly tired of doors being shut in his face. Lonn sat in the living room, out of Llias' line of sight, as music drifted through the open doorway. It was not the melancholy tune from the morning, but a complex, fluid, expressive melody that matched his mood perfectly. Lonn let it wash over him, sitting and staring into nothing, the refrain of Llias' music wrapping around his heart.

Lonn sighed. He could not avoid his own thoughts forever, much as he might like to. He was pleased by his morning with Llias, but he still had a lot to learn about courtship and the art of wooing. He had never had to do it before, having always either paid for company of his liking or taken one of the many, many offers that came his way. As long as he maintained no long-term dalliances and made no untoward promises, his parents did not trouble him about any of it.

His parents. That was another thing weighing on his mind. He was keeping Llias' identity as his familiar secret from his mother, and he had no idea how long he would be able to maintain that ruse. Surely she would sense some change in his magic before long. His father too, and he was even more dangerous because of his adamant refusal to consider any plan of action that did not end with the death of Vell's children. Lonn would not bow to his demand, but again, he did not know how long he would be able to resist. He needed to find another way forward, but he had too much spinning and circling in his mind to be able to think straight.

Secrets piled on problems piled on troubles piled on worries.

Illt, and the threat she posed to Llias was Lonn's biggest worry. Here in the heart of the palace Llias was safe, but even walking into the city was riskier than Lonn liked. Lonn's arm ached, as it did every time he thought of her binding spell. He would not give her Vell's children either. He would do nothing to harm the children he was uncle to, no matter what their nature, their appearance, and what the prophecies foretold about them. He would not.

A rough caw from the balcony caught Lonn's attention, breaking into his spiraling thoughts. The same raven from the previous day drew lazy circles in the air, the energy field preventing it from landing. Lonn watched it, curious; he had never known a raven come to his rooms. Vell had tamed a few in the royal forest when he was younger, befriending them with crumbs and seeds and bringing them back to the palace perched on his shoulders. They all flew off eventually, but some returned from time to time, visiting Vell's balcony and demanding to be fed. The thought of his brother snagged in Lonn's mind, and he found the controller and flipped the containment field off. The raven cawed again and landed on the low wall, looking at Lonn with a keen light in its gaze.

"What are you doing here?" Lonn asked the bird, its bright eyes and glossy feathers drawing him in. He cast about for something to feed it but came up with nothing. The housekeepers kept his rooms spotless, and he didn't even have a crumb to spare.

He went to Llias' door and tapped on the frame, glad to be distracted from his worries. "Llias," he called quietly, "I am sorry to disturb you, do you by chance have any food in there?"

Llias appeared, the lute in his hand, his brow furrowed. "Food? The crown prince of Otharn has to beg for scraps from his own prisoner?"

Lonn pointed at the raven sitting on the wall of the balcony, her shimmering black feathers almost purple in Foubla's light. Llias' eyes widened and he ducked back into his room. Lonn could not help but peek inside. The room had been transformed in just one day, and a cheerful clutter covered every surface. Clothes tumbled over the chair, books were piled on the desk, a set of knives in a wooden box rested on the floor, and a straight bow leaned against the wall. Llias and Darrin had been busy, but Lonn could not see any more before Llias was back, a half-eaten bread roll in his hand.

Lonn smiled at him, recognizing the sweetbread from the cafe in the city. "Has that been in your pocket all morning?" he asked, as he tore off a small morsel and gave the rest back.

"Oh hush, Your Majesty," Llias said with a sarcastic bow. He followed him out to the balcony, "We don't all know where our next meal is coming from every day, you see."

Lonn held out the scrap of bread to the raven. She took it and cawed in his ear, then rubbed her sharp beak on his shoulder before taking off and swooping over the city. She flew without stopping, out over the walls, heading for her roost. Lonn watched her go, food in her beak, free to fly where she pleased, to land and roost where she wanted, to associate with whomever she liked.

"I will never let you go hungry, Llias," he said.

Llias leaned next to him, the raven now just a speck in the distance.

"I know." He sighed, and turned to face the prince. "You're not a bad guy, Lonn. You're really not. You were right the other day, when you said I liked you. I do like you."

Lonn could hear the "but" on the tip of Llias' tongue, yet he didn't say anything more. He had already said his piece that day, and there was nothing more to add. The next move belonged to Lonn.

"What's this?" Llias asked, looking down over the wall at the energy crystals that powered the containment field. Before Lonn could reply, Llias reached over the wall to touch the nearest one. Lonn was too far away to stop him. He lunged towards Llias and grabbed his arm, but he was too late.

Llias' fingers brushed the unshielded crystal. Instantly, the energy discharged, ripping up through Llias' arm and into his body. Llias was flung back, slamming into the wall behind him, his head hitting the stone with a sickening thud that Lonn felt in his own bones.

"Llias!" Lonn cried, falling to his knees by the limp body. He shouted, "Guard! Guard!"

The outer door burst open a moment later and Hilde and Varla ran through, swords drawn, Erla on their heels.

"Fetch a healer," Lonn ordered. The girl paled and ran out, faster than either of the guards to react to Lonn's command.

Lonn cradled Llias in his arms. His pulse was weak and fluttering, his eyes closed, his face pale. Worse, their bond was fading. The ribbons and threads of arcane power that entwined them were breaking, twisting and stretching out of Lonn's control. He tried to hold on to them, but they poured through his fingers like water.

"No, no, no," Lonn moaned.

He ripped Llias' shirt open and put his hands on his bare skin, just as Llias had done to him in the training ring on Tornatt. He tried to force their bond to sustain, tried to push energy into him, but it was not enough. It was as though Llias were falling away, and Lonn was helpless to catch him, his fists closing on nothing but empty air.

There was no time to wait for the healer. Lonn knew what he had to do. He tore his own shirt off and held Llias, skin to skin. He poured every scrap of arcane energy his heart could summon into the unconscious man, wrapping him in it, filling him with it, forcing his heart to beat and his lungs to draw air, forcing his blood to pump and his injuries to heal. Lonn had no training in healing magic, and he certainly had no natural affinity for it. He had no skill to manipulate the energy of the crystal realm with his mind, but this spell came entirely from his heart; it needed no crafting, no complex structure or thoughtful casting. His magic knew its purpose, and it did as Lonn desperately begged it to do. It healed Llias.

"Urgh," Llias mumbled, awakening to find himself folded in Lonn's arms, both of them half undressed, Hilde and Varla watching wide-eyed from the doorway. "Lonn, what's happening?" he asked blinking in the afternoon light, utterly confused.

"Llias!" Lonn said, holding him around the shoulders, his fingers pressed into Llias' bare skin. "You are well? Are you in any pain?"

Llias sat up, unsuccessfully trying to extricate himself from Lonn's grip. "I'm fine. I feel fine. What happened?"

"The crystals," Lonn explained incoherently, relief fuzzing his mind while his panic drained away. "You touched one and it...Llias, thank the fates you are all right!"

Lonn clasped Llias to his chest again, overwhelmed with relief. This time, cleared of fear and panic, the touch of Llias' skin sparked an entirely different sensation. Llias gasped and grabbed Lonn's shirt, pulling him closer, the flush on his cheeks proof that he felt it too. The rush and spark and tingle of magic flowed through them both. Lonn bit his lip and caught an answering surge of desire in Llias' eyes.

"Leave us," Lonn ordered the guard without turning around.

Hilde managed a token protest. "My prince, the healer—"

"Have her wait," Lonn ordered, and repeated, "Out!"

The guards fled, shutting the inner door behind them. Lonn stared at Llias, no longer holding him but lightly touching his pale blue chest. Llias mirrored his gesture, letting his fingers trail over Lonn's skin. The light brushes of his fingertips drew answering surges of arcane energy through Lonn's body, bubbling inside him like the water from the hot spring where they had bathed together.

"Llias," Lonn said, his voice strangled. "Llias, I am not asking you to stop, but if you continue touching me, it will soon be very obvious how much I am enjoying it."

Llias smirked as his thumbs circled Lonn's crinkled nipples. "So, this is a bonus of the magical bond?" he asked, letting the back of his hand trail down Lonn's belly, leaving heat and sparks in its wake and a helpless moan on Lonn's lips.

Lonn nodded. "Yes," he whispered, squirming under Llias' touch, his pants uncomfortably tight. "I felt it when I first touched you, and it has only grown since then. Do you...do you feel it too?"

Llias looked up, his eyes so dark they were almost black, his cheeks pale mauve, his lips full and flushed. "I do," he confessed. "I do, but Lonn, I meant what I said today. I will not return your affections until you grant me my freedom."

Lonn set his hands on Llias' chest and slowly pushed him down onto his back, giving him all the time in the worlds to protest, to resist, but he did not. "You do not have to reciprocate, Llias. Is that not what you said? You will not *return* my affection?" he said, his voice low, rough with his arousal. His fingers dipped lower, stroking under the waistband of Llias' pants, and if his intent was not clear enough, he lowered his head to lick a long, slow stripe down Llias' belly.

Llias writhed and gasped. "You are serious?"

Lonn let Llias feel his weight, crushing him to the tile. Every spot they touched was afire with arcane sparks, the current running through them both, joining them and heating them, sending caution far from their minds.

"Yes," Lonn managed to pant out, "Yes, if that is your desire as well."

His palms were flat on Llias' chest as he worked his way down his body, kissing and licking his skin until he again reached the waistband of his pants. He paused, waiting, looking up at Llias while balancing on his word, the energy between them poised like a cat ready to pounce.

Llias made him wait, their eyes locked. Lonn could see the indecision in Llias' eyes, weighing the moment, temptation battling against wariness. Lonn was determined that temptation should win, so he brought Llias' hand to his mouth, licked the tip of his thumb then sucked it, swirling his tongue around before letting it slide out from his lips with a pop.

Llias groaned as his internal battle was lost, and he grabbed a handful of Lonn's hair, pulling his head down. "Go on then," he said. "Go on then, if you want it so much."

Lonn willingly went where Llias wanted him. He yanked Llias' newly tailored pants open, sending buttons flying across the floor. The flow of energy between them was no longer a river, but a torrent, a flood that threatened to sweep all before it. Lonn ducked his head and found the treasure he sought. Llias' cock was blue like the rest of him except at the head, where the blue turned purple, violet, the evidence of his eager arousal clear. Llias' hands tightened in his hair as Lonn licked up the length of it, the taste on his tongue divine — a combination of musky arousal and shimmering, sparkling magical energy.

"Suck it," Llias ordered, giving up on hiding his enthusiasm.

He was breathless, his fist tight in Lonn's hair and his other hand stroking his own hard length. Lonn growled and bristled at Llias' tone, but at the same time, an undercurrent of thrilled outrage sparked through him. How dare Llias speak to him in such a manner, to order him to perform for him? But he dared, and Lonn found that some deep, hidden part of him liked it. He braced his hands on Llias' hips. He was sure Llias was not going to give him an easy time, but he didn't care. He didn't care for anything but the taste of Llias' arousal on his tongue, the intense, fizzing sensation of his magic rushing through his blood, bubbling in his mouth like sparkling wine as Llias pulled his head down and pushed inside.

Lonn could not help the moan that vibrated in his throat at that, and in response Llias pulled his hair harder, which made him moan again as Llias let out a breathless laugh.

"You like that, huh?" he said, pushing his hips forward. Lonn could do nothing but tip his head back to find an accommodating angle and let Llias do what he wanted. The thrill of their connection was overwhelming, too powerful, pulsing through every cell of Lonn's body. Llias' hands yanked at his hair, his cock leapt in his mouth, and a trembling storm of arousal slammed into Lonn's belly. He let go of Llias' hip and shoved his hand in his own pants to stroke himself. A few moments later, he and Llias both reached their state of bliss together.

A concussive thud and crash rang out. Lonn instinctively threw himself over Llias' body, protecting him. The main door slammed open for the second time. Hilde and Varla appeared again, swords drawn, Erla and the royal healer close behind.

They all piled into a crowd in the arched doorway, confused at the sight of their disheveled prince lying on top of Llias, both of them half-dressed, sweaty, flushed and smiling.

Hilde recovered herself first, checking over the wall of the balcony while Varla checked the rest of the rooms. Llias grinned and winked at them both, giving them a lazy salute from his position on the floor underneath Lonn. The healer pursed her lips and sorted through her bag, pretending not to see anything out of the ordinary.

The guards checked the rooms, but Lonn already knew what had happened: The surge of energy between him and Llias had exploded the crystals that powered the containment field.

# Advice

The guards had to return to the balcony, and Llias glowered in frustration as Lonn ordered it done. Llias might have allowed Lonn's affections but Lonn certainly did not trust him to stay if there was an easy escape route open to him.

Llias folded his arms and stomped back to his room, leaving Lonn with his confused guards and the intoxicating taste of Llias' pleasure on his tongue.

Lonn had not yet recovered his equilibrium when there was a sharp knock on his door a few minutes later. Erla immediately opened it without waiting for Lonn's response, and he could see why when she performed her usual one-handed curtsy. His mother was standing in the reception room behind her, two of her ladies on either side of her.

"My prince," Erla said in her best formal-announcement tone, "Her Highness Queen Anlira awaits your pleasure."

"Mother!" Lonn said, shocked to see her out of her garden. The hem of her dress was stained with grass and specks of soil; she had clearly hurried directly from that place. "What is wrong?"

Anlira strode into the living room and cupped Lonn's face in her hands, looking searchingly into his eyes.

"What just happened?" she demanded, "I felt the disruption in your energy from deep in my garden. What caused it?"

"Ah," Lonn said, trying to will himself not to blush. He would rather not explain to his mother what he and Llias had been doing to cause that level of energy pulse. "It was nothing, Mother," he said, trying to squirm out from her hands. "That is, my...companion injured himself, and I healed him. That is all."

"Your companion?" Anlira asked with a frown, and then remembered. "That Fryst man you brought back from Tornatt? You still have him here?"

"Yes, Mother," Lonn said with a sigh, resigning himself to a lecture about appropriate princely behavior, but to his surprise he did not get one. Instead, he got a suspicious glare from the queen's narrowed eyes.

"I would like to meet this companion of yours," she said, and Lonn's immediate reaction was to refuse. He wanted to keep Llias out of his parent's awareness for as long as possible.

"Of course," he said, knowing that outright denial would only make his mother more suspicious. "He is resting now, and the healer is waiting to see him. I will bring him to meet you when he is recovered."

Lonn could sense Llias' awareness; interested energy thrummed through their link. For once Lonn did not embrace it. Instead, he tried to dull it down and hide it. He did not want his mother to sense anything unusual and start demanding answers.

Lonn prayed to the fates that Llias would not decide to indulge his curiosity and open his door. If he came face to face with the queen, there would be no hiding the truth of what he was.

Anlira hummed in thought and laid her fingers on Lonn's arm, sending a familiar tendril of her magic into his body. It was a guardian spell that Lonn remembered from his childhood; it had been soothing and comforting then, but now it felt invasive and unwelcome. He snatched his arm away, the ache of Illt's oath flaring up at the touch of the queen's enchantment.

"Mother!" he protested. "Stop that. I am no child anymore, to be settled down to sleep."

The queen smiled at that, the tension easing from her face. "You are still *my* child, Lonn. I worry about you, that is all. Come, walk with me back to my gardens."

Lonn took her arm and escorted her from his rooms, her ladies trailing silently behind them. He was glad to be heading away from his rooms and away from Llias. They passed Erla and the healer waiting in the reception room, and he paused to ask the healer to check on Llias when he woke up.

After he had bid his mother farewell at the entrance to her gardens, Lonn decided to check in on Darrin. He headed for his friend's rooms, hoping to find him residing there in comfort once more, not forced to hide out in the guardroom. Darrin had done a lot for him for him in the past few years, from finding his enslaved brother on Vaaladir, assisting David Thomen on Otharn and now acting as a friend and companion to Llias.

Darrin answered the door, surprised to see the prince calling on him.

"Welcome, my friend!" he said, gesturing him in.

Darrin's rooms were almost as spacious than Lonn's, but in a less desirable location. His quarters were not high in a tower with views overlooking the city, but in the back of the palace, with no balcony and small windows. Despite that, the rooms were welcoming and cozy, with scattered pillows and glowing lamps, low couches grouped around large tables for conversation and entertainment. Lonn had spent many hours here in years gone by, drinking, talking and gaming.

Lonn threw himself into his favorite chair with a long groan, the familiar comfort of Darrin's rooms feeling almost like a second home.

"Llias has been more *amenable* today?" Darrin inquired with a knowing look as he settled on the couch opposite.

Lonn covered his face with his palm. "How did you know? It is uncanny how you always know such things, Darrin."

His friend laughed. "I have told you many times, you cannot lie, and you cannot keep a secret! Both terrible weaknesses for a prince. I can always tell when you have been" —he paused to grin and clear his throat— "*entertained*, because the constant cloud of stress and worry that follows you around retreats for a while. Not long, mind you...but Llias has warmed to you?"

Lonn scowled. "He showed me what I was missing out on, by keeping him prisoner." He shook his head at the thought that he could be so easily manipulated. It had worked, and now Lonn found himself longing for Llias' smile, for his easy companionship, and yes, his affection too.

"Tell me about him, then, this Fryst man who has you so entranced," Darrin said.

Lonn looked into the distance, his eyes unfocused, thinking of Llias. "It is as though he was made for me, Darrin," he confessed. "I feel his presence in my heart, I see him — and his eyes are like the suns, his smile is like the stars. Today he held my arm as we walked, and it was as though the stones were the softest clouds beneath my feet."

Darrin snorted, unimpressed. "Tell me about *him*," he repeated, rolling his eyes. "I already know you are a lovestruck fool just from looking at you. What of Llias himself?"

Lonn furrowed his brow, trying to think. What did he know of Llias, other than the way the Fryst man made him feel?

"He plays the lute," he said weakly, already suspecting where Darrin was going with this line of questioning. "And...he likes bread."

Darrin hummed. "Likes bread," he echoed, nodding thoughtfully, "Well, indeed my friend, I can see what has you so worked up. You also like bread. You two have much in common."

"Stop," Lonn complained. "Stop. I take your point. I am selfish and self-centered, and I know next to nothing about the man I am infatuated with."

Darrin laughed and shrugged, open handed. "Well, perhaps if you paid more attention to him, and less attention to yourself, you might find it easier to win him over."

"I shouldn't *have* to win him over," Lonn muttered under his breath, but Darrin was right, as he usually was in matters of the heart.

Lonn had been selfish, and he had not opened his eyes to the reality of Llias' situation. Llias was a prisoner, far from his home, alone and defenseless, in the thrall of a selfish prince. No wonder he would not return Lonn's affection without some promises from him in return. It was self-preservation, not stubbornness, that made Llias behave that way.

Lonn shook his head and stood again, too antsy to sit and talk. "Walk with me. It is time we got your axe back."

Darrin grinned and hurriedly pulled on his sky-blue cape, swishing it over shoulders with his usual panache. "Jjon Ul has it. The king gave it into his safekeeping, and he was delighted to have it, I can assure you."

Lonn frowned as they left his rooms. "What did you to him, anyway?" he asked, recalling that Darrin had mentioned Jjon Ul now disliked him more than ever.

Darrin waved his hand. "I did nothing! Lord Ul suffered a most unfortunate accident while your brother was here, resulting in him losing his hand. He blamed Vell for it, and since Vell is not here, I am a convenient target for his wrath."

"He lost his hand?" Lonn exclaimed. Surely Vell had had nothing to do with that. Had he?

As they walked, Darrin told him the tale of the snakebite and the mysteriously locked door that had resulted in Jjon Ul's loss.

"Why did he...?" Lonn asked, and then remembered they were out from the protective wards of his chambers. He rephrased the question to something less incriminating. "Why did Lord Ul blame my brother for his accident?"

"Probably because of Erla," Darrin said, and at Lonn's blank look he added, "Surely you have noticed she only has one hand?"

"Of course," Lonn replied, affronted. He had noticed that the day he met the girl, despite her efforts to hide it. "What does that have to do with Jjon Ul?"

Darrin told him her sorry tale as they walked the rest of the way: Erla's injury from the king's wards on Vell's rooms and Jjon Ul's subsequent treatment of her, accusing her of stealing, demoting her to a maid and taking away everything she had earned as Vell's page, even down to the room that she slept in.

Lonn hid his face in his hands. Of course Vell was responsible for Jjon's "accident". Of *course* he was. His brother was fiercely protective of those he cared about. Vell had abandoned his home, his family, his titles and fled Otharn to try to protect his daughter Jormuna. He had been driven half to madness in his desperation and tried to make a place for them both by force on Earth. Laying such a simple trap for Jjon Ul would be have been easy for him, and Lonn had no doubt he had done it.

Having gotten to know Erla, Lonn found himself entirely on Vell's side. Jjon Ul had deserved the punishment Vell had arranged for him. They arrived at Jjon's offices, and armed with his new knowledge, Lonn was considerably less diplomatic demanding the return of Darrin's axe that he might otherwise had been.

It took less than ten minutes for Jjon Ul to return it. He clearly did not want to, but the crown prince would not be denied and was in no mood to wait. Jjon's secretary scribbled down Lonn's every word, which he had no doubt would make its way into Jjon's report to his father. Lord Ul had not survived for so long as the palace seneschal by being careless with his record keeping. Lonn would have to explain his actions to his father, but as the king had ordered him to make use of Darrin to find Vell, Lonn was not concerned.

Darrin tossed the axe in his hand as they walked back though the open courtyards, spinning it and sending shards of light all over the walls and floors. Lonn was glad to see a little of the spirit returning to his friend's eyes, and satisfied to have at least one of his pile of cares dealt with: Darrin Gulna Oxi had his golden axe back.

Now, Lonn had a far more difficult problem to solve. Llias.

# Bargain

Lonn arrived back at his quarters to find Llias in the reception room playing *kas* with Captain Hilde, of all people. Lonn had not been surprised when Llias persuaded Varla and Myrun to spar with him, but he had never thought that Llias would be able to charm his stoical guard captain. It seemed he had, and the two of them sat over the circular carved board, the red and gold pieces laid out in a complex formation. Erla sat nearby, watching them play, a neglected book in her hand.

Lonn paused at the sight. For years, this reception room had been empty, a buffer between his personal rooms and the rest of the palace. In a mere few days Llias had turned it into a gateway instead. It was not, as Lonn had always feared, a place for those trying to take up Lonn's precious time to ambush him and demand his attention. It had become a place for friends, for pleasant company, for people to gather because they wanted to spend time there, not because Lonn was flexing his authority to make them wait.

Lonn blinked, his heart strangely heavy. He had thought himself content enough with his own company, but in that moment he realized how lonely he had been these past years. He had kept people at arms' length after Vell's downfall, even Darrin. He had lost one person he loved, and he had tried to shield himself from that pain again. But Llias had broken through his barriers without even trying, without even wanting to, and now it seemed that Lonn had friends.

Hilde noticed him standing in the doorway and jumped to her feet, followed by Erla, who stuffed her book behind a cushion on the couch she slept on.

"My prince," Hilde said as though she had only just now realized where she was, and was about to make excuses for her presence.

Lonn nodded at her, an irrepressible smile on his face. "Captain," he said, and then added, "Erla, Llias, don't let me interrupt you."

With that, he sat down on the couch opposite the *kas* board, and gestured for them to continue their game. After a moment of uncertainty they did so, and a few minutes after that they were all so absorbed in the game that any lingering awkwardness faded away. Erla fetched lunch a while later, her new sky-blue scarf ensuring that she had no need to wait in the kitchens. They all ate together, plates on their laps, Erla and Lonn advising Llias and Hilde on their tactics, taking sides and betting bread rolls on the outcome of the match.

In the end, Hilde won, but it was a close thing right up until the final moves. Erla collected the plate piled with bread rolls that she had won and took the rest of the empty plates back to the kitchens. Hilde regretfully announced she also had to leave and attend to her duties.

"Your turn, my prince," Llias said, pointing to the chair opposite him, already setting up the pieces on the board again.

The challenge was clear in his voice, and Lonn, of course, would not refuse a challenge. Trouble was, he was not a very good *kas* player. He lacked the patience for it, and he usually did not care to sit quietly for so long. Still, he took his place at the board as Llias held out his two fists for him to choose his side. Lonn chose the left fist and got the red *konu* pieces, leaving Llias with the black *matu* pieces. That suited Lonn; *konu* was strong, but slower, while *matu* was weaker but faster. Lonn made his first move, pushing one of his heavy armored warriors out to the center of the board.

"Will you tell me about yourself?" Lonn blurted out, all delicacy forgotten. "I...um...I realized today, or rather, I had it pointed out to me, that I know little about you, and I would like to get to know you better."

Llias didn't look up from the board. He made his move and then said, "You already have decided I am to be your lifetime companion, Lonn. Why are you curious now about such trifling details as who I am?" His tone was even, almost bored, and Lonn flinched at his words.

Llias was right, but he said it in a way that made Lonn seem at fault. Lonn knew that Llias was his lifetime companion; they were joined by their arcane bond. Llias was his familiar, and even *he* knew it, as much as he resisted it. Lonn took a calming breath and made his next move, hardly looking at the board.

"I simply wish to know you, Llias," he replied

Llias considered Lonn's request. "I want to be able to go out," he said in response. "To visit Darrin, or anyone else I want, to go into the city, or anywhere else. You can even keep your guards on me if you like. If you grant me that, I'll answer one question about myself."

Lonn's jaw ached with tension. The request was not unreasonable and granting it would put him in Llias' good graces, but the danger of it made Lonn want to deny him. Llias would be vulnerable if he were out without Lonn's protection. Illt had cast her shade into the steam rooms on the palace grounds. In the city, perhaps she could even appear in the flesh.

"Four guards," Lonn said eventually, "and five questions."

"Three and three," Llias countered immediately, and smiled at Lonn's frustrated nod. "It's a deal," he said, finally making his move on the *kas* board. "What do you want to know?"

"Tell me of your family," Lonn asked, starting with as broad a question as he dared. He made another move without much thought; *konu* did not have to be so careful in the opening moves as *matu*.

Llias frowned. "I don't have any family," he said, shutting down that line of questioning as easily as Lonn had opened it. He moved his pieces to flank Lonn's slower pieces, setting up an obvious trap. "My parents died when I was young, and I have no other relatives. Two more questions."

"I am sorry about your parents," Lonn said. "It must have been hard without them."

Llias shrugged. "It happens, when the winter is long and the food supplies run low. I was too young to remember them. They sent me with the last of their food to the temple, which is where I became *ishax-ha*."

There was that word again: *ishaxha*. Llias had been telling Lonn what he was since the day they had met, and Lonn had not cared enough to listen. But he would hear him now. The reception room faded into the background as Lonn focused on the board before him and the man opposite, intertwined with the web of their connection. The threads of magic wove themselves in delicate patterns as they moved their pieces and talked, a latticework of arcane energy that almost glowed in the corners of Lonn's eyes. It was their bond, growing stronger, and Lonn would do everything he could to encourage it.

He moved his piece, pushing it forward towards Llias' formation. "What is *ishaxha*?" he asked, his voice low.

Llias studied the board carefully and made his move before he answered, forcing Lonn to wait for his reply. "Fryst is a hostile place, in many ways. It is freezing cold, and the star, Lady Orlane, is distant and faint. You cannot farm there, not as you do here." Llias gestured through the inner door and over the balcony railing toward the farms and orchards surrounding them, the rich, fertile grounds that provided the city with food all year round. "But despite that, there is beauty there. The ice we live under is centuries old, as pure and hard and clear as diamond. The subterranean lakes are full of fish and plants, warmed not by Lady Orlane but by the deep volcanoes. Far underground are creatures that have never seen the sun, and secrets that even the temple masters do not wholly know. *Ishaxha* is how we survive there, Lonn. *Ishaxha* is how we keep the warm water flowing, how we keep the people fed, how we keep the great creatures out of the cities. *Ishaxha* means *tamer of ice*, and that is what I do." Llias' voice was low, and his eyes did not leave the *kas* board. He moved his pieces, not closing the trap as Lonn had expected, but sneaking behind Lonn's frontline to target the second layer of more valuable pieces behind.

Lonn sat in silence, his skin tingling, Llias' homesick sadness was palpable through the strands of magic around them. Lonn set his hand on the table, palm up next to the game board, and Llias took it, letting Lonn comfort him, despite him being the cause of his unhappiness.

"I will take you back there," Lonn promised, "when this danger is past. We can travel there together. I would love to see your world."

"It is winter," Llias said, noticing his hand clasped in Lonn's and pulling it away, going back to studying the board. "It is winter and I should be there. One more question."

Instead of his final question, Lonn said, "The first shipment of food was sent to Fryst." There was an update on that topic in the bundle of papers on his desk under the *halfor* statue, among the bills from Llias' shopping. "Perhaps soon you can help me better know what to send, what your people need."

Llias nodded. "I will," he said with a sigh. "If that is all I can do for my people, I will do it."

"I should send bread," Lonn said with a small smile. "If you think your people would like it as much as you do."

"I suppose Otharn is not all bad," Llias allowed with a wry smile. "You do make good bread here."

They sat in relative peace for a few minutes, the quiet click of the game pieces the only sound in the room, until Llias looked up from the board. "You have one more question," he reminded Lonn.

Lonn asked the most important question he could think of, the one that had been on the tip of his tongue all day. "Will you accompany me to the Kalkis Festival?"

Llias snorted, unimpressed. "That's your third question?" he asked, his hand flicking out to move his pieces almost without looking. "Lonn, you are a terrible negotiator. I thought princes were supposed to be better at this kind of thing." There was no bite to his words, though, and as soon as Lonn had moved his *kas* piece Llias nodded. "All right, I'll go with you."

Lonn's smile lit up the sky.

Llias made his final move on the *kas* board, then stood up and stretched. "Well, you have had your three questions, even if you did waste one of them, so I will be heading into the city with my escort. I believe I need a mask for the festival tomorrow, no?"

Lonn jumped to his feet. "I will come with you," he said, and at the sight of Llias' raised eyebrows he rephrased his statement to a question. "May I come with you?"

"You may not!" Llias said happily, heading to his room and pulling on a jacket. "I want my mask to be a surprise."

"You don't have any money," Lonn objected, following him back through the inner door and into the reception room again.

Llias turned on his heel and pulled a small box out of his jacket pocket. It said *Lady Kina* in golden letters on the top. He snapped it open to reveal an elaborate ruby ring, surrounded by glittering diamonds. "I am sure I can sell this for a few coins," he said, grinning at Lonn's wide-eyed stare. There was a bill from Lady Kina's jeweler on Lonn's desk at that very moment, and it was not a small one.

"Did you buy that two days ago?" Lonn asked, equally impressed at Llias' cleverness, and horrified at himself for not even checking what Llias had been spending his money on.

"No, *you* bought it," Llias said, spinning back around and heading for the outer door. "A very generous gift, thank you Lonn. I will be back before evening."

Llias opened the outer door and greeted the guards like old friends, declaring that they were headed into the city. Hilde was on duty by now, she caught Lonn's eye with a questioning look; he had no choice but to nod. He had made the bargain with Llias, and if Llias would take his escort, Lonn could not go back on it.

Llias turned again before they passed out of sight. "I will take Darrin with me," he said, which set Lonn's mind somewhat at ease.

When they were gone, Lonn looked down at the *kas* board in the newly silent reception room. He already missed the company of his familiar, even though the comfort of their arcane link remained, pulling on his heart like the needle of a compass. He was tempted to study the board and be ready with a winning strategy when Llias returned to finish the game. But he saw that he was too late. Llias' final move had been to capture Lonn's *lemja* piece, the heart and strength of the *konu* side.

Lonn had already been defeated.

# Kalkis

Lonn had not been so eager for the Kalkis Festival in years. His truce with Llias had not wavered. The Fryst man seemed content now to give Lonn time to consider his options, and in the meantime to socialize with Erla, Darrin and the guards. There was no repeat of their passionate balcony encounter, but Lonn found himself revisiting the memory when he was alone that night. He did not admit it, even to himself, but he hoped Kalkis, with its masks and liquor and music would perhaps lead to another such encounter. But even if it did not, he told himself, it would be a merry night, and he needed it more than he knew.

Llias had spent the afternoon in the reception room, as was his habit now. Lonn could hear him through the open inner door, talking with Erla, Varla and Myrun. Lonn would have liked to be with them, but Erla had subtly reminded him of the stack of papers on his desk, so he had decided to take an hour and go through them. The *halfor* statue was in danger of toppling over.

Erla had rapidly filled every gap in Lonn's life that he had never noticed he had. She not only ran his errands quickly and efficiently, but she left flowers in his rooms, brought his favorite lemon cakes warm from the kitchens, and ensured the housekeepers only came when he was out. She was quick, clever and confident. If Lonn had ever thought to choose a page for himself, he would have chosen someone older, quiet and dutiful, but he was glad he had Erla instead. She had been loyal to his brother, far beyond what could be expected, and Lonn would see her rewarded for that.

Erla still slept on a couch in the reception room, hiding her things in the cabinets there. Lonn could easily commandeer a room for her in the upper levels where the servants lived, but he found he wanted to keep her close. Just like Llias, Erla was his now, marked by her sky-blue headscarf, and Lonn did not want them to be separated.

It was early evening by the time Lonn had signed and sealed every-thing, including a truly eye-watering pile of invoices that Darrin and Llias had run up in the past few days. Lonn had stopped reviewing them after the first dozen and just signed the rest.

Relieved to be done, he poked his head into the reception room. "Llias, are you ready for this evening? Darrin will join us shortly to walk into the city, Sinugult is already setting. Erla, please deliver all these." He handed her the stack of signed invoices, adding, "And you can take the evening off after we leave."

Erla thanked him and hurried off on her task while Llias followed him back into the living room, his excitement bubbling up.

"Yes, yes, I've been ready all day, Lonn! Your prisoner is getting bored up here. It's festival time, no?"

They parted ways to ready themselves and met back in the main room, their masks in place. Llias' mask was a crescent moon, covering half his face with strings of orange pearls and amber. The other half of his face was painted with stars, his blue skin part of the effect. He was also wearing a beautiful embroidered coat that Lonn had not seen be-fore, and that probably explained the size of his tailoring bill. It was wo-ven with yellow and gold thread, a gold sunburst on one shoulder and beads of amber spilling down the sleeve and up over the collar. Lonn had never seen anything like it on Otharn; it must be a style from Fryst that Llias had had tailored for himself.

Lonn lost his breath at the sight of him, the bond between them thrumming more powerfully than ever, grown stronger with the re-laxing of Llias' guard. Llias must have felt it as he smirked at Lonn, smoothing the sunburst coat over his hips. He held his arms out and said, "Well?"

"Stunning," Lonn replied.

His own mask was glossy black, made from raven's feathers and jet, covering his entire face. Llias could not see it, but Lonn had painted his face with snowflakes and ice crystals, sparkling with silver flecks and iridescent powder. Lonn would surprise him later, when they first traded masks after Foubla had set.

*"Well, well, such handsome strangers."*

Darrin strode into the room, a cup in his hand, his clothes bright white except for Lonn's sky-blue cape, which he never took off. His golden axe was once more on his back, and his mask was a fantastical bird of white feathers, pearls and beads.

"Darrin!" Llias greeted him warmly, "you look spectacular. You both do! You Otharnians really go all out for this festival, no?"

They strolled together into the city, Lonn's five guards with them. The guards had changed out of their uniforms and wore masks and face paint too, to blend in with the festival crowds. The streets were busy, and the main square was alive. Everywhere there were people, music coming from every stage, and every cafe and bar was open and serving hot spiced wine. The city was finally able to release the tension of the king's ban on travel and the constant surveillance, and it seemed the people were going to make the most of it. Even the king himself could not dampen the excitement of the Kalkis Festival.

The great houses on the square had their main doors flung wide too, more music drifting out of them, their lower floors open to all. The air was heavy with the scent of wine and with merriment. Dancing had already started in the square, and the crystal lights around the fountain cast a riot of rainbow colors over the scene. It was dizzying, and Lonn could feel Llias' delight surging through their bond. His hand found Lonn's larger one as they walked. Lonn didn't remark on it, but the spark of energy that grew there kept him warm far more effectively than the cup of hot wine Darrin pressed into his other hand.

"Dance with me!" Llias demanded, pulling on Lonn's hand, dragging him to a marked-off area filled with merrymakers, near a group of musicians performing a lively song.

Lonn hung back, reticent, but when Darrin said, "I'll dance with you." Lonn immediately grabbed Llias' arm.

"No," he said, to his friend's amusement, "I will dance."

Darrin winked at Llias, pleased with himself. He easily found himself his own dance partner, a woman with elaborate braids wound with ribbons and a mask made of mirrors.

Llias pulled Lonn into the dance and laughed with joy at the music and the movement of people around them. Even as the dance took them to other partners, a circle of linked elbows spinning back to back, Lonn could feel the thread of his magic connecting him to Llias, stronger with every moment. The pulse of Llias' heart beat through the bond and into Lonn's chest in perfect rhythm with his own.

They joined hands again as the bells of the fountain chimed. Foubla was setting, the last glimmers of her light fading from the horizon. The fountain glowed, and the crystal lamps all flared at once, covering the town square in sparkling light. A great cheer went up from the crowd. The night festival had begun.

It was tradition to trade masks every hour after dark until no one could tell who anyone was, and no one could be blamed for kissing anyone they didn't know. Lonn took off his mask and Llias laughed with pleasure at his icy face paint, his tribute to Llias' home world. Llias took off his crescent moon mask and traded it for the mirror mask held out by Darrin's partner. Lonn traded his raven for an embroidered dragon, but before they could put their masks on again, Lonn pulled Llias close.

"It is customary to exchange a kiss at this time," he whispered, his lips close to Llias' ear. Llias glanced around, and sure enough, there was a lot of kissing going on; Darrin and his new friend were following the custom most enthusiastically.

Llias stood on his tiptoes, and for a shocked second Lonn thought he was going to oblige him. Instead he whispered back, "Did you decide to release me then, Lonn?"

Lonn groaned, wrapping Llias in his arms and lifting him off his feet, rocking him from side to side. "I could make you," he said, lustful, sure that Llias was well aware he would do no such thing. Llias just laughed.

"You won't," he said. "And you won't be getting any kisses from your prisoner, only from your free companion." He held onto Lonn's shoulders, letting himself be lifted and hugged, Lonn's face buried in his neck. Llias lowered his voice and added in a low whisper, directly into Lonn's ear, "But if you want to suck my cock later, I might allow it."

"Might?" Lonn laughed, ignoring the music starting up again. His full focus and attention was on Llias, a pleasurable weight in his arms, arcane power flowing around them, the loop almost closed, the connection strong and steady and thrilling. "Only *might*? Did I not please my prisoner well enough last time?"

Llias wriggled in Lonn's arms, pulling on his mirror mask and lowering his head to speak low in Lonn's ear. "You'll have to work *very* hard to please me, Lonn."

Lonn shivered at the promise in Llias' voice, teasing as he loved to do. The balance of power was entirely inverted between them as the prince begged his prisoner for his favor — for his affection, even for a kiss. Lonn didn't care. Llias would be his, and Lonn would give him whatever he desired, indulge him in whatever manner he wished. If Llias would only accept his destiny!

Lonn set Llias back on his feet and they danced again, spinning and whirling and always connected by the threads of Lonn's power. The connection was so strong that Lonn could almost see it now, bright gold in the corner of his eye, a thousand spinning threads all centered on his familiar, a silent hurricane of arcane magic with Llias at the center.

# Fortune

"Come!" Darrin called to them when the music was over. "Minra will tell your fortune."

Darrin's dancing partner, Minra, led them through the crowds to an empty table tucked in the corner of an open-air tavern. Darrin sat beside her, one arm around her waist as she produced a bag of bones and rattled it, her broad smile showing under Llias' crescent-moon mask that she now wore.

"Very well, my dears," she said, her tone light. "My new friend here tells me that you need the guidance of the fates. Let us see what they have to say, shall we?"

Lonn shot Darrin a glare, but as he was still wearing the dragon mask Darrin remained blissfully ignorant of it. Llias laughed and removed his mirror mask to take a sip of the cool, foamy ale the bartender brought to their table.

"Fate," he said, shaking his head, "Fate is all I hear about here, but fate holds little sway on Fryst. We trust to luck and the light of Lady Orlane."

"Ah, but you are not on Fryst now, my dear," Minra said with a tap of her fingers to the back of Llias' hand. "Fate rules on Otharn, whether you wish it or no."

Llias huffed, but he didn't argue. Lonn was amenable enough to having this woman tell their fortune. He had had his fortune told at every Kalkis he had attended, but usually the soothsayers had no more than a sliver of magical ability. No skilled sorcerer would waste their time with such antics, selling tall tales to drunken merrymakers for a few coins at a time. No, this was nothing but a performance, another entertainment for the revelers, and Lonn would enjoy it as such.

"So, what will it be, my dears? Past, present, or future? I can see all secrets...for the right price." Minra rattled her bag again, and Lonn smiled under his mask at her routine.

"The future," he said, digging into his pocket and pushing a few coins across the table. Minra used them to buy another round of drinks for their table. Payment was required for a fortune to be read, even between friends. It was tradition, and Kalkis was a night full of tradition.

"The future," Minra said, shaking her painted bones and holding out her hand again, getting into her stride. "The future is difficult to see. Many clouds linger yet before my eyes."

Darrin dug in his pockets this time and bought a plate of spice cakes from a passing seller. He broke off a piece and popped it into Minra's mouth, following by a kiss to her painted lips.

"Mmm," she said with another broad smile at Darrin. "A fine price for a fine future."

Across the table, Llias leaned forward, his deep blue eyes watching the woman as she shook her bag of bones.

"First time, lovey?" Minra asked, noticing his interest.

Llias nodded. "Indeed. First time I have seen a fortune teller as bewitching as you."

Minra barked out a laugh. "Such a charmer," she chuckled, looking back at Lonn. "I hardly need the bones to tell you that your future is linked with that one, twined together like the roots of a tree, like the vines of the—"

She tipped out her bag of tokens and stopped talking, her mouth hanging open. Every single bone had fallen painted side down. Their future was entirely blank.

"My, my," she said, gathering the bones again, trying to recover her routine. "My, my, lovies, I have never seen..." She threw them again, and the same thing happened. They all looked at each other.

Minra straightened up, dropping her soothsayer act and taking off the crescent mask, revealing her tan, freckled face and light brown eyes. "Who are you?" she asked, staring directly at Lonn, the only one of them who still had his mask on.

Lonn pushed his mask up, showing himself to the woman.

"Prince Lonn!" she said, startled but too concerned to be overly solicitous of his rank. She pointed at the blank bones, "This is not good," she said flatly. "Someone or something is meddling with your fate. Have you two crossed any powerful magic users lately?"

"The witch!" Llias said, but Lonn had an even worse thought.

"My father," he confessed. He had resisted his father's binding and refused the order to kill his brother's children. If that counted as angering a powerful magic user, Lonn had certainly done it.

"More than one?" Minra said, sorting through her bones and picking out the ones she wanted, her fingers quick and nimble.

At Lonn's terse nod, she carried on.

"Think of the witch first," she instructed, "Everything you know about her, everything she said to you and you said to her. Let her fill your mind."

Lonn closed his eyes and thought of Lady Illt, both as she used to be and as she was now, burned, disfigured and vengeful. Minra concentrated for a moment then threw the bones; every single one was blank.

"It's not her," she said, gathering them up again. "Do the same with your father." She paled a little as she realized just who Lonn's father was, but she didn't stop her work. At Lonn's nod, she threw again, to the same result. The painted bones tumbled and clacked on the wooden tabletop, but they all landed painted side down. All blank.

"It's not him," Minra said, looking between them sternly. "Don't tell me you have crossed so many magic users that you can't even keep a track of them?"

"There is no one else," Lonn protested, but Darrin chewed his lip and raised his hand.

"There's one more, my friend," he said, and Lonn looked at him, startled.

"Who?" he demanded, disbelieving, but Llias had already realized the answer.

"You," Llias said, one hand reaching for Lonn's jaw, his gentle touch sending a shock of power through Lonn's body. "You, Lonn. I have crossed you many times since we met. You can't deny it."

"That's not—" Lonn protested, but Minra had already gathered up her bones, waiting for Llias to think of Lonn.

Llias closed his eyes and nodded. Lonn could hardly stand to watch the painted tokens as they fell from the fortune teller's hand. His breath caught as they rolled and spun on the board.

Each one landed painted side up.

Llias and Lonn stared at the evidence before their eyes. "What does that mean?" Lonn demanded, his hand gripping Llias' shoulder tightly, as though fate could cleave them apart through Minra's bones and words.

Minra studied the spread of the bones. "It means that you are attempting to thwart fate," she said slowly, rubbing her finger across her painted lips. "People attempt to thwart fate all the time of course — spurned lovers, grieving parents, failed merchants, defeated soldiers. All of them would defy fate if they could, but none are strong enough. You, Prince Lonn, have the will and the strength to do it. Fate has ordained a path for you, and you are refusing to walk down it."

Lonn's head spun. "What will happen?" he asked, his mouth dry.

The fortune-teller spread her hands. "I cannot tell. As you have seen, the bones cannot read what is not there."

"What fate am I attempting to avoid, then?" he asked. As ridiculous as it was, he had been avoiding many things that could be considered foretold. He had avoided fulfilling Illt's oath, he had avoided his father's orders, he had deceived his mother about the nature of his relationship with Llias, hiding their familiar bond. It seems that since he had met the Fryst man, he had done nothing but avoid what others expected of him. Perhaps it was time he decided what he *wanted*, not what he wanted to avoid.

Minra studied the bones that lay on the table, her eyes intent, tracing the pattern they made with her fingertips, muttering under her breath. She pulled three out of the spread and set them before Lonn and Llias. "These three are the most powerful," she said. "I can't remember a time I have seen them all show their faces in one throw."

Llias picked one up and flipped it over and over in his fingers. "You said it was fate that we met," he told Lonn, the painting of the joined worlds on the token appearing and vanishing in a blur of motion.

"I did," Lonn said, looking at the other two bones Minra had indicated, a fang and a crown. A creeping feeling spawned in his gut; he knew exactly what they meant. The vision that his mother so feared and that had sent his brother to his torment: the sundering of the joined worlds.

He *was* attempting to avoid that fate, of course he was. It was his duty, and he intended to fulfill it. He just would not do it by killing the children. He would find another way. He picked up the fang, leaving the crown token on the table.

Minra's sharp gaze followed his movement. "Interesting," she said. "I would have thought you would choose differently, Prince Lonn."

Lonn shrugged. "My head is not ready for a crown," he said, showing a moment of rare vulnerability before this woman that he had just met. But Lonn felt that he'd grown to know her well in this short time. Darrin clearly already adored her, sitting close to her side with his arm around her slender waist.

"The fang is a powerful rune," she said, gesturing to the bone Lonn held. "It is the web of life that was here before us and will be here after us. The spirits of water, air and land dwell in the fang, and so does the power of those outside the bonds of civilization. Beasts, but also beastlike men; thieves, killers, and worse."

They sat in silence for a moment, the noise of the festival dulled around them, all their focus on the bones.

"I see from your face that you know more than you wish to discuss," Minra said eventually, gathering up the tokens and putting them back in her pouch. "That is your business, but beware, Prince Lonn. Those who try to thwart fate often wish they had faced it instead."

"No," Lonn said, putting the fang token back on the table with a soft click. "If I face fate, it will be to defeat it. There is no other choice."

# Orange Blossom and the Arcane Heart

"So you're thwarting fate, huh?" Llias said when they were alone again. "Does this have something to do with the witch Illt, and your brother Vell?"

Llias still did not know the full story of what had happened to Lonn's brother. He had gathered that it was nothing good, and that Lonn's parents were behind it. Lonn's warning not to reveal himself had gained an important context, and Llias now agreed that staying beneath the notice of the king and queen was a good idea. An even better idea would be to get off Otharn entirely, of course, but he was still working on that plan.

Lonn was deep in thought and didn't reply, so Llias dipped his hand into the prince's pocket and bought them both a cup of spiced wine from a nearby booth. Perhaps they should just drink and be merry for the rest of the festival. Whatever Minra's dire warning meant, it would still be waiting for them tomorrow morning. Lonn took the cup and drank it down, handing it back to Llias absentmindedly. Llias shrugged and bought him another one.

This time, Lonn pulled him close when he took the cup, squeezing him in his arms with a needy groan. Llias let him do it; he had no reason to object. Lonn had been amenable all day, and if he were to be honest, Llias was getting accustomed to his affection. He breathed in the smell of him — wine and leather and that maddening scent of orange blossom Llias knew was not really there. Since the day before on the balcony, Llias had been occasionally distracted by wandering daydreams of Lonn: his smile, the heat of his mouth, the sound of his breathy moan calling out Llias' name.

As if responding to his thoughts, Lonn nuzzled into Llias' neck, sending a shiver of anticipation down his spine. The gentle brush of his lips on Llias' skin was both a suggestion and a needy request.

"Llias," Lonn breathed in his ear, pressing their bodies together. He hesitated for a moment before he added, "Llias, would you care to accompany me to that dark alleyway over there? You will find me most accommodating."

Llias snorted out a laugh. The prince had certainly made good on the promise to be surprising, and Llias liked that about him. When Lonn abandoned the conception of his rank and station and let his guard down, he was sincere, genuine, passionate and not at all full of himself. Llias reached up and cupped his jaw between his hands, looking into his electric blue eyes, the dark pupils deep enough to drown in. Lonn bit back a moan at his touch, and the soft buzz of magic tingled on Llias' palms. By now he had realized that Lonn felt it far more intensely than he did. Llias felt a thrill of power, just as he had on the balcony when Lonn had been so eager for the pleasure of sucking him.

He slipped one hand under Lonn's shirt. The quivering tension of the muscles he found there was like that of a stallion about to run, a bull about to charge, yet entirely at Llias' command. He swallowed his increasing desire and said, "No to the dark alleyway, if it's all the same to you, but if you think we can find a room…"

He needed say no more. Lonn grinned and grabbed his hand, dragging him to the nearest tavern. They sneaked past the raucous taproom and crept up the back stairs. They had put their masks back on for this criminal endeavor, breathless with suppressed laughter at their juvenile behavior. They tried the doors on the upper level until they found one that was open and fell through it into a bedroom, empty but for the bag resting by the door. Whoever had paid for the room must be out enjoying the festivities, and they likely would not return for hours. Perfect.

The only light came from the city square below the window, and Llias pushed it open to allow the music, laughter and merry cheers to float up to them. The dim light was enough for him to see Lonn waiting for him in the center of the room. He had taken his dragon mask off, running his hand through his dark blond hair, but that was all.

"How do you want me?" he asked, and Llias was on him, pulling at his shirt before he even thought about it.

"Undressed," he said. "I want you undressed, my handsome prince."

Lonn was eager to obey, and Llias left him to it and started on his own clothes. He dropped everything on the floor and tumbled Lonn onto the bed the moment they both were done.

"Lonn," Llias gasped, rolling on top of him, stretching out, relishing the heat of his skin, the warm press of his eager arousal against his belly.

Lonn's eyes rolled back in his head, a breathy, desperate moan passing his lips. He wrapped his arms around Llias, holding him as close as possible, lost in the delight of his arcane power's reaction to Llias' presence. Llias was certain he could do whatever he liked at that moment. Lonn's pleasure would only grow the more he was touched; he would be the easiest and most receptive partner Llias had ever had. Despite the wicked spark of temptation at the thought, Llias would not let himself take advantage of their bond in such a way. He sat up, pulling away from Lonn enough to allow him to recover his senses.

"No," Lonn moaned, trying to pull him back down. "Llias, come back!"

"I will, I will," Llias said, unable to keep the delighted smile off his face at Lonn's impatience. "But first, tell me what you want."

"Anything," Lonn said at once. "Anything, anything, just come back here."

"Anything?" Llias said, with a bite to Lonn's shoulder that got his attention. "I would think a prince should be more careful with his promises."

Lonn's eyes focused on Llias' face, his senses returning a little with the reduced contact. "Not with you." Reaching up, he brushed a strand of Llias' midnight-blue hair back from his temple. "Not with you, Llias. I know what fate Minra said that I am resisting, and it is not this one.

It is not you and I. We met by fate and we are joined by fate. So, tell me what will please you, and I will do it."

Llias swallowed, all thoughts of his plans and strategies gone from his mind. Only this moment remained: Lonn naked in his arms, giving himself freely, willingly. How could Llias not do the same?

"I want to fuck you," he panted, not yet touching Lonn. He wanted to hear him say yes without the force of his magic clouding his senses.

Lonn grinned, wild and exhilarated, just as if he were flying. "You're going to make me lose my mind," he said. When Llias still did not move, he added, "Yes! Yes, come on, what are you waiting for?"

Llias scrambled off the bed and dumped out the bag of the luckless room-owner, praying he would find what he was looking for. Lady Orlane must have been listening, because he seized a small bottle of oil as it fell out and jumped back onto the bed, holding up his prize. He popped the cork and the room filled with the heavy scent of orange blossom.

The oil. Llias looked at it dumbly, noticing the illustration of the orange tree painted on the bottle. *Fate*, he thought, *Damn Otharnians and their fate.*

But then Lonn pulled at him with a pleading look, and Llias didn't even care about fate anymore. He tipped out a handful of the oil and spread it all over Lonn's chest and arms, lying on top of him and spreading it over himself too. He let the slickness cover their skin, writhing together until Llias reached down and stroked Lonn's cock with one long, tight stroke. Lonn was already too far gone to speak. The sound that came from his mouth was almost a scream of pleasure — a wild gasp, wordless and intense. All Llias wanted to do was hear it again.

He tipped out more oil and slipped his fingers further down, as Lonn made room for him, spreading his legs on instinct alone. Again he was lost in the intensity of his arcane power reacting to Llias' touch. Llias could feel it too now, the tingle building to a pulsing beat, throbbing against his skin in time with the pounding of his heart. He stroked his fingers around the tight furl of Lonn's muscle and the prince moaned, wrapping his legs around Llias' hips and trying to pull him in, his hands stroking Llias' skin wherever he could reach. Lonn was drunk on Llias' touch, and Llias was overcome with a wave of desire as he looked down at him. Lonn trusted him with this, he wanted it, he gave himself willingly, holding nothing back.

Llias would hold nothing back either, he thought, he would give Lonn what he wanted. They were both covered in the oil now, the heady scent of orange blossom dizzying in the room. Llias was glad he had opened the window, or he would be just as lost as Lonn. The smell triggered his deepest memories — the magical underground temple and its sacred spring where he learned the deepest secrets of his world as he was now learning the secrets of Lonn's body.

The air around them vibrated with power as Llias gave up on preparation and let Lonn have what he so clearly needed. He tried to take it slowly, but Lonn was impatient, eager, hungry for Llias' cock.

What chance did Llias have to resist? He could not, and he sank into Lonn's body with one deep thrust, both of them entwined about each other, slick with oil and drunk with passion and with the strength of their connection. The threads of arcane power snapped into place, linking and joining together as Lonn and Llias moved in unison, the power flowing between them, the circle connected, their arcane heart finally united. The vortex of power was closed and looping, flowing endlessly with Lonn and Llias in the eye of it, in the center of the storm, riding it to their crashing climax.

# Discovery

Lonn opened his eyes to a world of light. Everything glowed, and he blinked, confused. The metal fixtures in the stolen bedroom sparked with arcane power, but that was nothing compared to the brightness streaming through the open window. Lonn disentangled himself from Llias with an exhausted groan and rolled off the bed. He staggered to the window and looked out, dreading what he would see. The main square was dazzling. Every crystal decoration blazed with light, brighter than daylight, each one pulsing in rhythm with the beat of Lonn's heart. It was what had happened to the containment crystals on Lonn's balcony, but a hundred times more intense.

"Oh..." he said, struck dumb by the sight and by the aftershocks of his climax, his skin still alive with the sensations Llias had drawn out of him.

"Oh no, was that us?" Llias said, coming up behind him.

Llias was slightly more alert, but not much. He leaned on Lonn's back and gazed out of the window, his skin warm and exceedingly distracting. Lonn nodded. This was not good, but he was having trouble remembering why.

"Well, I suppose no one's going to think I'm your infatuated little plaything now, are they?" Llias asked, and Lonn's heart stopped. Llias was right. They had exposed their secret and revealed the true nature of their relationship to anyone with arcane senses in the entire city, including Lonn's parents.

Fear was like a sudden bucket of cold water dumped over Lonn's head. "We have to get back to the palace," he snapped. He pulled on his pants and threw Llias' golden jacket at him. "Get dressed, hurry."

Hand in hand, they hurried down the back stairs. The lamps that had been a dim glow on their way up were now radiating heat and light, too bright to look at. They tumbled out onto the square, Lonn frantically searching the crowd for Hilde and his guards. Where were they?

Lonn had been a fool; he should not even have come to his festival. The risk was too great, and he had made Llias a target.

*"Lonn!"*

The hiss came from behind them, and Lonn turned, relief flooding through him at the sight of Darrin hand-in-hand with Minra. Minra's lipstick was smeared and Darrin's shirt open, half the buttons missing.

"Is this your doing?" Darrin asked, gesturing to the spectacular lights all around them.

Before Lonn could answer, the shining *fjarleoth* in the center of the square dimmed as its excess of power was syphoned away. There was a sharp crack and a deep black shadow spread on the ground. A moment later, Queen Anlira herself stepped through the travel stone, her eyes blazing gold with anger. She looked directly at the alleyway where Lonn and Llias stood, her fingertips sparking with the effort of travelling against the current of Lonn's energy.

"Lonn," she said, her voice low but carrying throughout the square, bouncing from every crystal gem like a shivering, tinkling echo. "Lonn, come to me now."

"Darrin?" Lonn whispered.

He did not dare to look away from the incensed queen. Her face was bright and terrifying as her power rose around her, a twisted net of light and air, strong and beautiful as a spider's web.

"Yes," Darrin said, grabbing Llias' arm and pulling him away. "Yes, understood."

Lonn stepped out from the alley, ignoring Llias' protest. Lonn would face his mother, and Darrin and Llias would run in the other direction and stay safe.

"Where is he?" Anlira demanded as Lonn walked towards her. "Where is this companion of yours? You have deceived me; you have hidden the truth from me at this most critical time! The prophecies swarm through my dreams and their meaning is hidden by your lies." The filaments of the queen's power floated in the air around them, glinting and sparking from the discharge of Lonn's magic. She dragged a shaking hand through her hair, pulling strands from her crown braid, as uncontrolled as Lonn had ever seen her.

"Who is he?" she asked. "What is he? What power does he have over you?"

Lonn kept walking, heading out alone into the center of the square, putting more distance between him and Llias' hopeful escape. He did not bother to deny anything. The city square was alight with the evidence of his guilt, and all he wanted now was for Llias to get away, back to the warded protection of Lonn's chambers.

Anlira grabbed Lonn's arm in a vicelike grip and sent a twist of her guardian magic through him. It was the same spell she had used the day before, only this time far more powerful, scouring Lonn down to his core and finding not just his connection with Llias, but also the oath magic Illt had bound him with.

"What is this?" the queen again demanded. She jabbed at Illt's spell, trying to peel it away from him. "What spell has that poisonous enchanter cast on you?"

Her son reacted before he could even think about it. It was as easy as breathing to let his mother's magic slide off him, to shield himself and draw on the strength of his bond to do it, the connection humming through every cell in his body.

"Llias is my arcane familiar, Mother," Lonn said. "He is the companion of my heart, and he has cast no spells on me."

He kept his voice calm and even. He needed to stall the queen and give Darrin time to get Llias away. Lonn was strong now, stronger than he had ever been, but his mother was far older and wiser in the arcane arts than him. Llias was not yet safe, and neither was he.

The square was as bright as daylight but eerily silent. The festival revelers were pressed back to the walls, urgently pushing their way out of the square and back down the side streets. They were hindered by the curious crowds behind them that wanted to get closer.

"Impossible!" the queen spat. "Do not entertain such foolishness. That man is not your familiar. I would have seen it. I would have known. He has tricked you, worked some sorcery on you."

"Then why did you not see *that*?" Lonn shot back. "Why did you not see such trickery, if that if what you claim it to be?"

The light in the queen's eyes dimmed, but she shook her head and recovered a few seconds later. "He has concealed his workings," she said, utter certainty in her voice.

"Is it so easy, then?" Lonn said, uneasy fear gnawing at his belly. "Is it so easy to cloud your sight? To manipulate what fate shows you, and what you tell the king? Who else has hidden secrets from you, guided your visions and turned your eyes away from the truth?"

"Be silent!" Anlira snapped. "You do not understand what you are speaking of. You are not ready for such power. You are too young, and you have no training. I will end this matter for you."

Behind her, the *fjarleoth* dimmed again as the queen's guard stepped through, the energy level finally low enough for them to travel safely. They stood around their queen, warriors and mages both. Behind him, Lonn sensed the solid presence of Hilde, Ake, Nife, Myrun and Varla, facing off against the queen's guard, ready and willing to defend their prince against whatever threat arose. Lonn's heart swelled at their loyalty, but he raised his hand in caution. They would find no victory if they took up arms against the queen.

"Where is he?" Anlira demanded again, ignoring Lonn's guards. "Surrender him to me and no harm will come to him."

Lonn shook his head. "I cannot do that, Mother."

"You must," Anlira said, gesturing to her guard to search the alley from which Lonn had emerged. Lonn didn't look over his shoulder, praying to fate that Darrin and Llias were gone already. Darrin knew the streets of the city well; he knew the alleys and shortcuts and every tavern courtyard with an unlocked back gate between here and the palace. He would be almost there by now, surely.

"Captain, take your soldiers and return to barracks," Lonn ordered in an undertone. This was not going to end well, and he did not want his guards in the middle of it. He could not shield them from his mother's wrath. He was not sure he would even be able to shield himself from it.

Hilde ignored him, standing behind his shoulder with her hand on the hilt of her weapon.

"Hilde, that is an order," Lonn said, not breaking eye contact with his mother.

After a few breathless moments, Hilde gave a terse nod and stepped back. She and the others melted away into the crowds. They would not return to the barracks, but at least they were out of the queen's sight. That was the best Lonn could do, for now.

The queen's guard captain emerged from the alley with a shake of his head. Llias and Darrin were gone.

The queen strangled her snarl of rage, and Lonn suppressed every scrap of his connection to Llias. He buried it all in the depths of his heart so that the trail could not be followed, and so that Llias would not be given away by Lonn's feelings for him.

"Where is he? Bring him to me at once!" Anlira ordered, her voice crackling like lightning, the crystals around her dimming and flickering, their power absorbed into her web. "You will defy me no more, Lonn. Make your choice now: Bring him to me, or I will find him myself and you will never see him again. This is an order from your queen."

It was as Minra had said. Fate would not be thwarted; it could only be faced. And it was time for Lonn to face it. He made his choice.

"No," Lonn said simply, summoning Skarpur to his hand. "Your Majesty, Llias is mine, and I will not give him up."

With that, Lonn kicked off from the ground, but the queen's magic followed him like a striking snake, biting into his flesh and pulling him back down. Despite Lonn's efforts to suppress it, his link with Llias surged and the queen sensed it. Her eyes lit up again, flat gold, and Lonn knew he had little time.

He gave up on subtlety and opened his heart to the connection. He was flooded at once with strength, his own power returned to him in a steady pulse, clean and direct, and with it Lonn wiped away the sticky threads of the queen's restraints.

He kicked off from the ground again, and this time he flew.

# The Knife Edge

Lonn threw himself into the air, his power unfurling around him like a flag. Flying towards Llias was as easy as falling into his midnight eyes. It was as though Llias were Sinugult and he were Foubla, bound together by gravity and destiny. Nothing would keep them apart. No prophesy or power of his mother's or even of his father's would stand in their way. It was fate.

He landed on his balcony, as light as a feather. Llias was there with Darrin, his festival attire exchanged for dark, practical clothes with no adornments, his weapons on his back.

"Lonn," Llias said in a tone that brooked no argument. "We are leaving."

He emptied the last of the jewelry bags Erla had delivered in the past few days and stuffed gold and gems into his pockets, handing what didn't fit to Darrin.

"Yes," Lonn said, striding towards him and wrapping him in his arms, smothering his startled *oof* against a shoulder. "Yes, Llias, we are leaving. I should never have brought you here, and I apologize for doing so. My parents are blind to everything but my mother's prophecies. They can see nothing else. They will not listen to me, just as they did not listen to Vell. They are too far gone in their own beliefs."

Lonn ran to his room to change out of his festival clothes and collect what supplies he needed. He picked up a sturdy chest of gold and silver adornments he never wore and dumped it in Darrin's arms.

"You must leave the city," he said. "Find Erla and take her too. Tell Hilde, as I am sure she has plans for such a thing. She was always far-sighted."

"Aye," Darrin said. "Do not worry about Erla and me. Minra owns a vineyard outside the city, and she invited me to join her."

Lonn smiled at his friend, glad that the night was not filled entirely with bad news. "A beautiful woman who owns her own vineyard? You were lucky to run into her tonight."

"Luck?" Llias said with a smirk. "Perhaps it was fate."

"Perhaps," Darrin said with a smile, holding out his arms to them both. "I think Minra was unsurprised to meet me tonight, and you as well, Lonn. She is a fortune teller, after all."

"Make haste," Lonn said, after enveloping Darrin in a crushing hug. "You must be gone before my mother arrives. She will not be more than a few minutes behind me."

"Aye," Darrin said again, backing towards the door, the heavy chest under his arm. "But where will *you* go?"

As he spoke, the raven that had visited them twice before landed on the balcony with a loud caw. They all stared as the bird spread its wings and cocked its head at them, a pine needle in its beak. Its black eyes gleamed with something more than animal intelligence.

Darrin broke the silence with a whisper, "Vell…"

"Go, do not say another word," Lonn snapped, the truth coming over him in a wave.

He all but shoved Darrin out of the heavy outer door and locked it behind him. Of course, *of course*. The royal forest, full of tall, majestic pines. The raven was a messenger, and Lonn had been too stupid to notice it. Vell had always loved the forest. He had found himself an abandoned cabin in its hidden heart, spending days and nights there, going alone as often as he had gone with Lonn. Whenever Lonn had visited his father's observatory at those times, Vell's crystal lens had been blurred and clouded. Covl had explained it to him once — something about the flow and balance of power, but Lonn hadn't cared, and he had forgotten it until now.

Vell and his children had never left Otharn. They were hiding in the royal forest, and Lonn was going to find them.

Lonn grabbed Llias, his spear still in his other hand. Time slowed at the touch of his familiar, their bond solid and strong, humming between them. Lonn's power was more stable and responsive than it had ever been.

"Llias, tell me now if you want to leave. I'll drop you at the travel portal and you can go back to Fryst, or anywhere else you want. You're not my prisoner, and you're free to go."

Before Llias could reply, a crash echoed through the outer door and the wood shuddered as though struck with a ram. There were very few people who could break the wards on the royal chambers, and fewer still who would dare try. Lonn knew who stood at his door, and so did Llias.

"Oh no," Llias said, with mock indignance. "You're not getting rid of me so easily. You think you can discard me now, after you've had your way with me?"

Lonn laughed and grabbed him firmly around the waist as another blow hit the door. The crystal lamps in the room sputtered and dimmed as arcane power was drawn from the wards.

"I am glad," he said, pressing a kiss to Llias' neck and ignoring the crash. It was the sound of his prior life ending, and a new one beginning. "But I think it was you who had your way with me, not the other way around."

Llias had no time to reply, as with a final shuddering crash the door broke, and the queen's guard burst through. Anlira entered behind them, her eyes glowing with crystal light, a small golden harp in her hands.

"Lonn!" she called, her voice like music, twining around Lonn's nerves as her fingers moved on the strings. "My son, please do not take this path. Your father only wants what is best for you, and for the joined worlds."

Lonn's power faltered and he shook his head, trying to clear it. Anlira's music muddled his mind, smothering him in her will like the softest of blankets. He struggled to keep his own thoughts in his head, chased away by the queen's whispers.

*...rest, my son. Your mind is troubled, let me help you. I will take care of you. I can ease your worries, just give your companion to me, he is not worthy of you...*

"Focus," Llias hissed in Lonn's ear.

His warm hand slipped under the collar of Lonn's shirt, his palm on Lonn's shoulder, skin to skin. The cobwebs cleared at his touch — and just like that, Anlira's music became discordant, ugly, and tuneless, her soothing words nothing but lies. Lonn shivered, sick to his stomach. How often had his mother ensorcelled him in such a way? She used to sing him to sleep when he was a boy, her harp in her lap, granting him peaceful dreams, or so Lonn had thought.

"We're leaving," Lonn said, backing away towards the balcony, Llias by his side. "Do not try to stop us."

"Lonn, you do not understand what you are doing," Anlira said, reasoning with him as though Lonn had not just at that moment caught her trying to cast a spell on him. "This is a critical juncture. Many prophecies converge on this point. If you leave with him, you will send the joined worlds down the darkest of paths!"

"No!" Lonn snapped, warmth and comfort pouring into him from Llias' hand, lending him strength. "No, you are wrong, Mother. You were wrong about Vell, you are wrong about his children, and you are wrong about Llias. I will take my own path from now on. I am done with your lies."

"Vell's children are—" Anlira interrupted, the light burning in her eyes, the strands of hair that escaped from her braid floating around her head like spider-thread.

"They are monsters, yes I am aware!" Lonn retorted, furious now, every lie and manipulation of his parents coming back tenfold: the long years without his brother, the trickery, the lies, and now the threat to

Llias. He would not tolerate it any longer. "They are monsters, but they are your grandchildren, Mother. Perhaps it runs in the family."

With that, Lonn turned and wrapped his arm around Llias' waist. He raised Skarpur and leapt, the queen's outraged shriek echoing behind them. They flew like an arrow from Llias' bow, out over the city. The music and laughter of the Kalkis revelries faded away as they soared into the silent darkness beyond the walls, together.

# Epilogue

"So, we're fugitives now?"

Llias was sitting on the porch of the forest cabin, enjoying the morning air, checking his arrows and not-so-subtly watching Lonn chop wood.

"We are," Lonn said simply, dragging the last of the fallen logs into the clearing.

They had found the cabin just as Lonn remembered it, nestled in the valley under a rocky outcrop, deep in the heart of the royal forest. It had been protected by Vell's wards in the long years since anyone had been there, and it was well stocked and cozy. The night before, they had just slept, exhausted from their encounter with Anlira, from the wild flight out of the city, from fear and exhilaration.

That morning, Lonn had decided the mindless exercise of chopping logs was just what he needed to clear his head. He had not cut the wood of the living trees; Vell had often warned him that the forest was guarded by spirits who would punish anyone who tried that. Lonn didn't know whether he believed the warning, but there was enough fallen wood for him not to tempt his luck. He already had a pile of cut logs, and now he was ready to split them.

He raised his axe.

"You should lose the shirt," Llias said, his tone overly casual, belied by his dark gaze.

Lonn paused, the axe above his head. Then he shrugged and let the long-handled axe *thunk* into the tree stump he was using to split the logs on. He pulled his shirt off and tossed it onto the porch next to Llias without a word. Llias' satisfied smile was like the suns on his skin as Lonn picked up the axe again.

"Do you have any plans, other than to hide out here and show off your biceps?" Llias asked, timing his words exactly as Lonn swung the axe down.

The blade stuck in the wood, and Lonn glared at Llias as he wrestled it free. "You…" he started, but Llias was grinning at him, white teeth against full, blue, lips, and Lonn found he had no choice but to smile back. He set the log up again and got back in position. "My plan," he said, swinging the axe and splitting the log, turning it and splitting it again, making perfect wedges for their open hearth, "is to wait here until my brother comes. Then we will all decide together what to do next."

Llias ran his fingers up the length of one of his arrows and spun it in his hand in a blur of motion. "He'll find us here?"

"He *invited* us here." Lonn nodded, thinking of the raven with the pine needle in its beak. "We are surrounded by his wards, and I am sure he already knows where we are. We will not have to wait long."

Llias nodded back and set the arrow down before taking the next. He had twelve arrows in the quiver he had escaped with, as well as his bow and his *tanda*. It was enough for them to hunt game for a while, if they were careful and retrieved the arrows after each shot. The cabin was stocked with flour and grain in magically sealed containers, as well as tools such as the axe Lonn was using now. It was a cozy place, and it felt safe, protected by the depth of the forest and the encircling wards. The tension that lingered in Lonn's jaw was easing away, even though he was now, as Llias had pointed out, a fugitive.

"I am sorry I dragged you into this," Lonn said.

To his surprise Llias merely looked thoughtful.

"It was not your fault," he said, tapping the fletching of his arrow against his lips. "It was Illt who took me from Fryst, and you who saved me from her. You are not the one who should apologize."

"I could have let you go," Lonn insisted, bringing the axe down again.

Llias shrugged. "You *could* have been less of an ass about it, but you were right. Illt would not have let it end there, even if you had let me go. Her plans are intertwined with your parent's plans, no?"

Lonn nodded. He still had not been able to speak of the price Illt had demanded of him, but Llias was too clever to much doubt what it was.

Llias continued, "She would have used me as a weapon against you. At least this way my people got the supplies you shipped."

"They will keep getting supplies for a while," Lonn said. "At least until the merchants notice their bills are not getting paid."

Llias rested the arrow on his fingertip, checking its balance, then set it down and took another. "You're slacking off," he said, pointing with his arrow at the woodpile.

Lonn rolled his eyes, but he got back to work. Sinugult's morning light filtered through the branches of the trees, warming the air of the clearing. For a while, there was no sound but the bite of the axe and the susurration of the wind in the pines, rising and falling like the waves on the ocean. Lonn lost himself in his task, falling into an easy rhythm, splitting log after log until he was surprised to find there were no more logs to split. He looked up at Llias, who was leaning forward on the porch, his arrows forgotten, his eyes dark and intent.

Lonn decided that Llias had had enough of a show, and it was time for him to provide some entertainment of his own.

"Come with me," Lonn said, throwing down his axe.

He pulled Llias into the cabin by the arm and rolled him onto the bed. Llias wriggled out from under him, complaining at his hot, sweaty skin, but it was a token protest. He could have squirmed free if he wanted to, but he clearly did not, letting Lonn manhandle him until he was sitting astride the prince in the narrow bed.

Lonn grinned up at him. "I knew you'd sit on my lap, eventually."

Llias groaned at Lonn's smug look.

"You are insufferable," he said, rummaging in the pocket of his jacket and producing a small, corked bottle. "And you are lucky that I remembered to bring this."

He flicked the cork out and the sweet, tantalizing scent of orange blossom filled the cabin. The fragrance was heavy with meaning in both their minds.

"I *am* lucky," Lonn replied, his hands tight on Llias' hips, looking up at him with darkening eyes. "I know that now. I'm the luckiest man in the joined worlds."

Llias smiled and leaned down to kiss his prince — soft and sweet and tender.

# Before you go

Mailing List

Sign up to my mailing list for short stories, advance chapters, and updates.

[www.carolinegibsonbooks.com](http://www.carolinegibsonbooks.com)[1]

Also by Caroline Gibson

Thrall Prince Romance – ebook and paperback

Prince for Sale (Book one)[2]

The Prince's Fate (Book two)[3]

The Arcane Heart (Book three)[4]

Thrall Prince Romance – audiobook

Prince for Sale (Book one)[5]

The Prince's Fate (Book two)[6]


1. http://www.carolinegibsonbooks.com

2. https://www.amazon.com/dp/B07KDQ72J3

3. https://www.amazon.com/gp/product/B07V64WHXY

4. https://www.amazon.com/dp/B07YYN1VH3

5. https://www.audible.com/pd/B07Q1K3PZD/?source_code=AUDFP-WS0223189MWT-BK-ACX0-147260&ref=acx_bty_BK_ACX0_147260_rh_us

6. https://www.audible.com/pd/B0816SLGWX/?source_code=AUDFP-WS0223189MWT-BK-ACX0-171448&ref=acx_bty_BK_ACX0_171448_rh_us